YOUR BOSS SAYS HI

INDIE SPARKS

DEDICATION

The illustrated boss on the adorable cover of this book has not prepared you for Daddy Thick Thighs. But don't worry. Hollis is fully able to introduce himself (and his thighs) on the page. I could tell you a specific page number, but then you would go straight there and skip important things that happen before he drops his jeans. You'll just have to trust me that he's going to drop them soon, but he's quite the gifted giver, so when I tell you not to skip the things that happen before the unveiling of his thighs, you'll want to follow those instructions. Start on page one, but be prepared for page—

You'll see.

CONTENTS

ONE

HOW IT STARTED

Christian never made it any secret he thought he was smarter than me. His accomplishments were always bigger, his job more important, his plans more logical . . . but he must take me for a complete idiot if he thinks he can gaslight me into believing I didn't get a clear look at that image on his phone. Raw and uncensored. If he hadn't ripped it out of my hand and hit delete faster than a politician leaving a whorehouse, I'd have that shameless shot on my own phone now as permanent evidence.

"How long have you been fucking her?"

"Oakley, come on. It was just some random girl from the internet. You know my brother sends me that shit all the time. I hadn't even seen that one yet."

"Right. Some random girl with the same cross-eyed squirrel inked on her shoulder and bangs so choppy they look like her busted tattoo came to life and chewed them off!" There is not enough tequila in Texas for me to have misinterpreted that picture.

"Okay, now you're just being mean. Her tattoo is not that bad."

"Yeah, I'm sure she has no *ragrets*! You cheating, sack of shit, fuck boy!"

"Jesus, will you calm down? I already told you that picture wasn't who you think it was. Your jealousy makes you paranoid. It's not a good look, babe."

"Can you hear the words coming out of your mouth?" The last thing I want to do is make a scene at his company picnic, but if I don't put some distance between us right now, he'll be leaving this corporate circus in an ambulance. And I'll be going out in handcuffs. It's a good time for another trip to the margarita machine.

Carnival games line the grassy lawn of the Nyx International campus, everything from old-fashioned options like ring toss and balloon darts to electronic basketball hoops and a virtual reality quest of some sort. As I walk, I consider which ones I might want to play to occupy my time and keep me away from Christian. What's the point? Could I actually enjoy anything right now?

Getting railed by a stranger in this sundress.

Shut up, tequila.

There is something delicious about angry sex, though. I let it play out in my mind for a moment, a revenge fuck I can throw in his face before we split the silverware . . . like it would really make me feel better to bang one of his coworkers just because he's doing one of mine.

Anyway, the silverware all belongs to me. We won't be splitting a damn thing from that drawer.

When I tell him I'm taking the silverware, he'll grab the barbecue tools. I'll say the painted champagne glasses are mine because they were a gift from my mom, and he'll say I better not even think about taking the Waterford crystal goblets his mom gave us, or the beer steins his dad got for him in Germany. Always with the one-upmanship. So predictable. I can already see exactly how this will go: I'll take one thing, and he'll claim something he considers bigger and better.

Christian values labels and prestige above all else. He always has. Notwithstanding his current skank-ass, low-rent side piece, obviously.

But it's never been monetary value that made something matter more to me. I'm sentimental. A fucking sap. That's how I conned myself into staying in this broken relationship for so long. I should order an Uber and get out of here.

There's no reason to run out before having one last free margarita, though. That's something I could enjoy. Besides, I already walked all the way over here.

Hollis Nyx, President and CEO, leans on the end of the bar with his crisp white shirtsleeves rolled up onto his tatted forearms, watching his employees enjoy all that he's provided for their entertainment on this picture-perfect spring after-noon. He played for the Texans before he hung up his jersey and switched to button-downs, and while I know nothing about football, I know this man still works out. His jeans hug his thick legs—and oh, for the love of queso, do I want to massage that man's quads. With my inner thighs.

He lifts his cup and smiles in my direction as I approach. His square jawline is evident even through a perfectly trimmed beard—short enough to be professional, yet still a little rugged, and long enough to make me want to run the backs of my fingers over it. While I massage his quads. With my inner thighs.

Huh, what do you know? Suddenly I'm in the mood for a little one-upmanship of my own.

I smile his way and return the cup salute. As far as I'm concerned, my barely legal coworker and her tree-rat-infested shoulder can have Christian.

And his *Daddy Thick Thighs* boss can have me. I run my eyes over him and wonder what it would take. Pulling his fleeting attention is one thing, but could I pull more from him? He smiles at me again, and something in the tilt of his mouth makes me think maybe I could.

TWO

STEP INTO MY OFFICE

The bartender looks up and nods at my plastic cup. "Another margarita?"

"Yeah, thanks." I surrender the cup and try to sneak a glance at Hollis Nyx out of the corner of my eye. He catches me. Because he's staring right at me. That can't be right. He's probably just keeping an eye on the bar, making sure things are running smoothly. That's what he does. He runs things.

A fresh cup, overflowing with the frozen barely-boozy slush that counts as a margarita at these things, is set on the bar in front of me. There is no tip jar. The company is taking care of everything, including gratuities, so the employees and guests don't have to spend a dime out of their own pockets today. We are, however, supposed to turn in a drink ticket on every trip to the bar. Three per person to keep the company's liability in check, and I cashed in my third for my last cup.

The bartender's eyes flit from my face to the cup, and back again. *Dude, don't make it weird.* I pick up the cup and smile. "Thanks."

"Oh, I, um," the bartender stammers and halfheartedly gestures toward the cup that's already in my possession—

clearly, by law it's mine at this point—halting his hand in mid-air. "Do you have a drink ticket?"

"I already gave it to you." *Not technically a lie. I gave it to him about an hour ago.*

He blinks, slowly tilts his head like he's trying to decide if I'm joking. When I don't laugh or reach into my purse for the requested ticket, he says, "I'm really not supposed to let you take that without collecting a ticket."

"You did collect my ticket. When you took my empty cup." *An hour ago.*

"I don't think so." I can see he's questioning himself as he works through the scenario out loud. "My process is to make the drink and then collect the ticket when I deliver it."

"But that doesn't make any sense, does it? If you're not supposed to hand over a drink without a ticket, why would you make the drink first? Then what happens if the person doesn't have a ticket? You just waste the drink? That costs the company money. Is that how you were trained to do it?"

His expression is dumbfounded. "I'm an actual bartender. I work in a real bar, and that's the way we do it there, too. We don't make a customer pay before we give them the drink. They pay after."

"Don't most customers open a tab?"

"Some do, yeah."

"So, then they don't pay until the end of the night, when they're done drinking and ready to leave, right?"

"Right."

"Well, I'm not leaving yet, and you definitely took my last ticket, so open a tab for me in case I need another drink. We'll settle up when the party ends."

His gaze shifts warily from side-to-side, and then it goes straight to my tits. He finds my face again and smiles like we share a secret now. "My name's Dane. I'll take care of you."

Not in the way you're hoping, you won't. But that's cute. "Thanks, Dane."

I turn to find Daddy Thick Thighs (*Oof! Stop calling him that!*) definitely staring at me, slowly shaking his head, and smiling. He lifts his empty hand, extends his pointer finger toward me, and rolls it back in the universal *come here* sign. My eyes are transfixed on his finger, extending and rolling back, over and over again. I squeeze my thighs together but my clit still throbs with every stroke. How the hell am I supposed to walk over there like this? Then again, how the hell could I not go to him? It's like he's reeling me in, so I stop fighting it and let it happen. He's pushed his sunglasses up onto his head and his amber eyes are as shiny as his polished boots.

Everything about him is polished to perfection. "Hi," I manage. This cotton sundress suddenly feels too tight across my chest, rough against my nipples. Maybe it's the way my shoulders have snapped back. I'd relax them if I could, but nope, we're just going to stand at attention and await his inspection, I guess.

His eyes remain on my face. "Are you trying to get that bartender fired?"

"I would never." My eyes go wide.

He laughs. "I think never might be an exaggeration."

"Are you flirting with me or insulting me?" *Whoa, ease up on the defensive tone.* I take a sip of my drink, try to compose myself.

"Do you really think I would've called you over here to insult you?" He tips his beer back, watches for my response as he swallows.

I shrug, force a slight smile. "How would I know? I don't know you. I mean, I know who you are, but I don't know you."

"You have me at a disadvantage already. All I know about you is that you don't work here." He takes another swig from his cup. "That much I'm sure of, because I would've noticed you before now."

"No, I don't work for you." I bring my cup to my lips

again but he keeps staring, his eyebrows raised, waiting for me to say more. "I'm here with Christian Connolly."

His brows knit together, trying to place the name. He's rumored to know every employee's name. "IT department, right?"

Wow. I guess the rumors are true. "Yeah. He thinks very highly of you. You're sort of his idol."

Hollis grimaces. "Pretty sure I'd fall from grace if he knew how hard I've been eye-fucking his girl."

Excuse me, sir! I'm going to need you to define how hard exactly . . . "I'm not actually his girlfriend anymore. It's complicated. Anyway, he deserves worse. Trust me."

"I've always been a firm believer in giving people what they deserve. Trust me." The same finger he used to summon me traces the watercolor murmuration of swallows migrating down my inner forearm. "This is pretty. Do you have more?"

I turn and lift my hair to show him the vibrant, pixelated seahorse on the back of my neck. When his finger touches me there, it sends a ripple down my spine. His breath tickles the baby hairs that wisp above the seahorse as he leans closer and says, "Your artist does good work. Any others?"

"Not that I can show you without taking off this dress." I have no hidden tattoos, and I don't even know where that came from but my nerves are all lowkey vibrating right now so I guess he just rattled my inner tease. I can't believe he's touching me like this, looking me over, inspecting me for real. I turn around to face him again. We're so close I could count his eyelashes, if they weren't so damn lush. God, is everything about him thick? There goes my spine again. I swallow hard, knowing this is the moment to make my intentions clear— but do I have the guts? *Take the shot.* "But to be honest, I was kind of hoping to get railed while still wearing it."

His smile is devious, the glimmer in his eyes wicked, and the tone of his voice positively lurid. "Oh, you can absolutely leave the dress on. The first time, anyway."

Holy shit. How is this real? Maybe it's not. Tequila, the stress of discovering Christian's cheating, the sun . . . I could be hallucinating. Or passed out on the ground right now and this is a dream. All I know is if I'm blissfully blacked out and imagining this, I will kill the motherfucker who revives me. "Should we go for a walk?" I ask, mainly to be sure I'm conscious.

"Is that what you want? For me to lead you over that hill, force you to the ground, and grind permanent grass stains into this sexy-sweet sundress?" He toys with the thin straps as he talks.

Yep, you pretty much nailed that fantasy on the first try. I don't realize I'm nodding until he puts his hands on either side of my face to still me, and shakes his head no. His smile widens. "I was thinking of somewhere a little more private. Like my office, but I need to know something first."

"What?"

"Your name."

"Oakley."

"Oh, please tell me I'm going to find an Annie Oakley themed tattoo somewhere on your gorgeous body."

"That was my nickname in high school."

"Of course, it was. What about the tattoo?"

"Guess there's only one way for you to find out."

The rush of air-conditioning when we enter the building chills my whole body. No one is working today so the place is eerily quiet. Our breathing practically echoes in the silence as we wait for the elevator. I jump when the doors open. He presses his hand at the small of my back to guide me inside, and the doors close again. We are all alone now. Just me, him, and the ink on our skin.

THREE

ART FOR ART'S SAKE

Hollis's executive suite takes up an entire corner of the building, overlooking the wooded greenbelt on the backside. The building is only three stories, but the tall flowers that line the walkway to the trails look like nothing more than colorful dots in the distance, and the narrow creek that flows under the bridge is just a dark stripe bisecting the landscape. This office feels so impossibly removed from the cubicles where Christian and his coworkers spend their days. I've only seen pictures, but their workspaces are nothing like this. I'm both impressed and intimidated, and I'm not sure which I feel more.

The artwork on the walls is original. It seems odd that an artist would be moved to capture a pumpjack surrounded by scrub brush, but the subject seems worthy of the canvas with the pink sunset sky behind it. The longhorns grazing in a field and the running horses make more sense to me as art you'd hang on the wall, but it's not my office.

His desk is exactly what I would've imagined: expansive, dark wood. Solid. The kind of piece that won't give under the weight of paper or responsibilities. *Or me?* Hollis approaches from behind, pushes my hair aside, and kisses my neck. He smells good, like warm spices and fresh-cut grass. I couldn't tell outside over the comingled scents of beer, cotton candy, and barbecue, but in here, he settles a cloud of aromatherapy over my shoulders. "That's a beautiful desk."

"It's going to be significantly more beautiful in a minute." He scoops me up and carries me toward it, sets me down, facing his chair. I let my sandals fall to floor, expecting him to kick the chair out of the way, but he sits in it instead. "Pull your dress up around your waist and scoot your ass to the edge."

Oh, God. He's asking me to slide toward him while he watches? When I lift the material like he's asked, and fully expose myself, he releases a groan of appreciation. "Do you always leave your panties at home, Oakley?"

I'm not about to tell him that I've been trying anything I can think of to get Christian's attention lately, to shift things back into overdrive the way they used to be when he couldn't get enough of me. And I'm for sure not going to admit that my boyfriend probably wouldn't have bothered to find out if I was wearing underwear today or not.

All I had to do was enter his orbit and Hollis Nyx took notice, beckoned me closer. I stop when it feels like I'm at the edge but he grabs my hips and pulls me forward again. He parts me with his thumbs and takes in the sight of my bare pussy, spread open and dripping with arousal. I feel my warm juices run down my perineum, and I want to die right here on his desk. This is too much vulnerability, not the type of hard I wanted him to inflict.

But then he says, "Good God, you are exquisite." And I melt a little, feel my spine relax onto the wood until my fore-arms are hardly holding me up. He runs his tongue through my seam, curling at the top to swipe the tip of my clit. "Relax, sweetness. We're going to be here awhile. You taste entirely too good to rush."

His thumbs still hold me open while his tongue traces

patterns over my silken skin—crazy eights? his name?—and I flow like a fountain. He laps at me like he can't get enough. I'm flat on my back by the time he focuses on my clit, flickers his tongue over it and sucks playfully, but he keeps dipping back down to dart his tongue in and out of my pussy, and I can't help but buck my hips every time he does it. His mouth is back on my clit and he's sucking harder.

I'm close but he pulls off again, goes back to tongue-fucking me, and then he brings his mouth to my opening, practically sealing it against me, and his tongue does things inside me that I can't discern exactly, but I think I might come with no attention being paid to my clit at all, which would be a first for me. But he stops again, goes back to my clit and licks and sucks. *Oh, God, he's probably getting so annoyed with me.* "I'm sorry," I blurt.

"What's wrong?"

"I take forever sometimes. And you're doing so much and you're really, really good at it. It's me, not you. It feels amazing and I'm trying, I promise."

He hoists his body up over mine, balancing his weight on his hands, which causes the veins on the sides of his neck to surge at the surface. His beard is damp and glistening. He brings his face close to mine. "You don't apologize for feeling pleasure. Anyone who ever made you feel like you needed to hurry, like you were on his goddamn clock didn't deserve to have his mouth or his hands on you to begin with. Look at me."

My breath is caught in my lungs and tears strain the backs of my eyes, and I don't know if I want to cry because of all the bad stuff with Christian or this one incredible moment with his boss. I don't even know this man. I can't possibly want to cry because of him, but I think I might.

Hollis is enraged, but the words leaving his mouth are adoring and validating. "I'm enjoying you. Making you feel good is not something to get out of the way so I can get on with shoving my dick inside you. Your orgasm is more than a precursor to mine. Make no mistake, unless you object, I am going to fuck you and you're going to know you've been fucked when I'm done. But right now, I am nowhere near ready to stop tasting you. And just so we're clear, I know when you're close. If anybody's being tortured here, it ain't me." He winks, and then he kisses me, hard and aggressive at first but he slows, and his tongue mimics the maneuvers it's performed between my legs.

When he breaks the kiss, he smiles down at me and says, "Can you imagine anything else in the world tasting that good? People try to compare it to other things, like fruit, but if there was a fruit that tasted like that, farmers would raze their crops and plant whatever magical vines could bear the delicacy. Whole farmers markets full of nothing but snatchberries and cunteloupes and . . . " He smiles when I burst into laughter, try to cover his mouth with my hand, and beg him to stop.

Who makes jokes like that? A man who's trying to put an anxious woman at ease does. Hollis Nyx does. And it's worked.

"Yeah, there she is," he says, stroking my hair. "That pretty girl in the sundress, the one with her hair blowing in the breeze, and that dazzling smile that took my breath away. Lie back, beautiful. Let me do this right, because I've got a bad feeling no one else ever has. And I don't like feeling bad. Be a good girl and relax. Don't interrupt me again."

FOUR

SO, TELL ME ABOUT YOURSELF

It's not hard at all to do as Hollis has asked, to leisurely lie back and let him take his time, to let myself enjoy it without worrying about how long he's had his face between my legs. No pressure on me to react in a timely manner. But I would've never been able to relax like this if he hadn't said those things to me. I guess he's not one to sugarcoat anything, just boldly says what he thinks. I've always loved dirty talk in the heat of the moment, but it's different coming from him. Dirty, but somehow reverent at the same time.

His mouth is hot, and everything down there is insanely wet, including his beard at this point, I'm sure, but I don't feel self-conscious about it, just brazenly aware. Between the groans he's releasing and the sloppy sounds of his mouth on me now, this is downright filthy. And I'm living for it.

I thought my legs were as far open as they could go, but something releases and they butterfly wider. He lifts my hips, and the shifting angle gives his tongue access to a switch that increases the sensitivity of every nerve ending in my body. My resolve shatters and tumbles like pieces in a kaleidoscope, and I see all the colors behind my eyelids as I fly apart. I always thought a woman screaming a man's name when she comes was something that only happens in movies and books, but Hollis's office fills with my voice releasing his on a current of breathy shrieks. He holds on to me until my body stops quaking. I open my eyes to look down at him, and I have never seen a more gorgeous man in my life.

He helps me off his desk and lifts my dress over my head. My legs are shaky but they keep me upright. His eyes take in my naked body as he takes a step back. I watch as he unbuttons his shirt and peels it off his sculpted shoulders and down his arms, revealing his brick wall of a chest, black tattoos everywhere, perfectly lined and shaded. I could stare at them for hours. He's a living, breathing work of art.

He carries me to the huge leather couch and lays me on my side. I shiver when he unbuckles his belt, and a knowing smile spreads across his face. I'm only slightly embarrassed that my eagerness to see his cock is so blatantly revealed. When he sits on the coffee table in front of me to remove his boots, he maintains eye contact, and I'm getting more anxious by the second to have his hands back on my skin, to feel the heat of his body against mine.

When he stands again, it's to shove his jeans down over his hips, and as the denim goes lower, those muscled thighs that have become his defining physical attribute for me come into view. Once the pants are on the floor, the only thing covering the mass of his erection is his black boxer briefs, and to say it appears to be straining to break free is an understatement.

Hollis steps forward, and I reach out to do the honors. And fuck me, it is an honor. Calling a guy's dick his manhood always sounded so prudish to my ears, but this? This is manhood personified. *Damn, speaking of art.*

I stroke him and he moans. I make a similar sound as the girth of him tests the flexibility of my jaw. Pulling my mouth off, I swirl my tongue over the swollen head and spread his pre-cum to coat it well before I slide back down the length until the tip touches the back of my throat, threatening to trip my gag reflex. I breathe through it, relax for him, but he buries his fingers in my hair and moves me off him again. "As good as that feels, I'm not done exploring you yet."

I shift back to make room for him on the couch. The cushions sink under the weight of him, rolling me closer as he settles in. His broad shoulder blocks the sunlight streaming in through the window while his hand roams down the length of my body and back up again. He pauses to palm my breast, and pinches my nipple. "You like this?"

"They're sensitive."

"They're supposed to be." He releases the hardened peak and lets his thumb brush over it a few times, causing my shoulders to tense. "I think somebody has control issues."

"I think somebody only recognizes that because he has them, too." My fingers glide through his hair.

His laughter is soft. "Guilty. But you can relinquish control to me. I won't hurt you. I promise."

"Well, if that's the deal, then I'm leaving. Where's my dress?" I push myself up as if I want off the couch, but he pulls me back down. We both laugh, and he continues to graze my nipple with his thumb while I try not to shrink back with every pass.

"So, you want gentleness here," he says, dipping his head to kiss my nipple. He draws it into his warm mouth and sucks lightly before he brings his face up to look at me again. "Where do you like it to hurt, Oakley?" His hand moves between my legs and he inserts two fingers in my drenched pussy, and then a third. "Is it here? Do you like the feeling of being stretched?" I bite my lip and nod, roll my hips. He hammers his fingers into me, his hand striking hard against me when he buries them to the third knuckle. "Do you like it a little rough?"

"A little."

"We'll get there." He kisses my cheek, and whispers in my ear, "What about that sweet ass?" I still against him, wholly unprepared for him to take a complete inventory of my boundaries. Is he really asking about anal when he's barely had his fingers in me? Before I can decide how I want to respond, he clarifies his question. "Do you like to be spanked, sweetness?"

My pussy clenches on his fingers, stealing my option to lie, or at least hedge my penchant for it. I'd already zoomed ahead to fretting over granting him backdoor access; the thought of his giant, stinging handprint on my ass got left on the starting line. I reverse back to the origin of the query, exhale, and confirm what he's probably already assumed. "Sometimes."

He kisses me like there is no world outside this office. No company event in full swing on the lawn, no major news breaking, no fault lines shifting or storm cells brewing, only us. Only this.

His fingers continue to probe and tease my pussy and I kiss him back like I don't know a world beyond this space either. I actually wish I didn't, which makes this more than a hookup; it's a hideaway, an escape. My legs quiver, and he speaks without fully breaking our kiss. His voice is raspy, practically growly, sending vibrations over my lips. "You know you're my private whore behind this closed door, right? And I may just decide to keep you." *Oh, okay. Just pry my spank bank wide open and steal the script.*

His thumb presses hard against my clit, and he bites down on my bottom lip. "Come for me like a good little slut. Make a mess on my hand like you did on my face. Show me how bad this tight, needy cunt wants my cock to ruin it for other men." His hard-on lurches against my leg, and my spine arches as my orgasm surges. I unravel completely for him again, this time whimpering his name into his mouth.

"Am I that transparent?" I ask, my body collapsing next to him as if my bones have become gelatin.

"Maybe I just know how to read you."

"I think that's a given."

He slips his fingers from my pussy and brings them first to his mouth, and then to mine. "Mmmm, you're very good at being bad, Oakley. And bad girls have to be punished."

We start to change our positions, but I'm thinking one way and he's going another. Before I know what's happened, he's sat up and is pulling me across his lap, face down. This is not what I expected. I thought I'd roll over and he'd lie next to me for this, keep it intimate and playful. Does he seriously think he's going to put me over his knee and spank me like legit corporal punishment? I don't know about this. I mean—*Oh, sweet mother of multiple orgasms! Give a girl a warning tap first, maybe?* My gasp elicits a villainous snicker from him.

Hollis Nyx is used to doing things his own way. He may take my parameters under advisement, but I know he's going to push them. And I'm absolutely going to let him.

FIVE

OPENING MY EYES

ollis's hand covers my entire butt cheek every time it comes down on one of them, whether it's to slap or to rub and knead in between. This is not punishment. There is pain, but it's interlaced with so much sensual touch that I look forward to the stinging slaps more than I ever have with anyone in the past.

Once again, he has me in a completely vulnerable position, and I don't do vulnerable—or I didn't before I entered this office. I actually like being on display for him. It's thrilling, powerful in a way that defies logic because he is so much bigger and stronger than me. Physically, I'm at his mercy right now, but letting him take the reins completely feels freeing.

I feel protected by this man who I shouldn't even be with, who is no doubt leaving marks on my body, who I know is turned on by the redness he's causing. At this point, there are probably welts rising along with the heat, but as long as he keeps soothing them, I don't care.

He slides his hand down between my legs and groans. "My goodness, you do enjoy being spanked." I was already obscenely wet from everything he'd done before, but when he moves his hand to part my legs, it becomes evident my thighs are slick. This whole scene is vulgar to the point of being pornographic. *Put this in a painting.* My only preference for how he fucks me is soon.

As though he can read my mind, he pulls me up to sit face-forward on his lap. His dick stands straight up between us and I want to lift my hips and impale myself on it. He smiles, twirls a section of my hair and stares at me like being able to read my current thoughts isn't enough, like he wants to read my memories, too. My slickened inner thighs hug his naked quads and it feels every bit as good as I'd imagined. I wantonly rock my hips, putting my need on blast.

He lifts me into position and keeps a loose grip on my waist, leaving me free to take him at my own pace. The engorged tip entering me is perfection, and I know I'm going to feel every inch of him stretching me, despite the abundance of natural lube my body is still churning out. *Damn, welcome to Oakley Falls.* My head lolls to the side as I slide down about halfway and pause. The fullness is already incredible. "Mmmm, that feels so good," I admit in a hushed tone. He pulls my body forward and takes my nipple into his mouth. The uncomfortable sensitivity is gone. His tongue circling, and then the force of his sucking is enough to make me want to stay right here. But before I even realize I'm doing it, I'm sliding to the base of his cock, taking him completely. It doesn't hinder his access to my nipple one bit. He makes sure of it.

I bury my fingers in his hair and pull his face closer, urging him to suck harder. He takes my cue and offers some prompting of his own by thrusting upward. I fuck him in short strokes, rubbing my swollen clit against his hardness, being selfish after all he's already given me, but he indulges me, doesn't force a shift in the momentum. His body is solid beneath me, patient as I get myself off and come on his dick, but the moment I'm done, he flips me over. Rising up onto his knees behind me, he pushes my shoulders down and pulls my ass up, positioning me exactly where he wants me, and then he fucks me every bit as hard and I knew he would. My cheek is smashed against the plush arm of the couch and sweat runs from my face onto the leather.

"You've been needing this for a while, haven't you? It's been too long since anybody's properly fucked this pretty little snatch, left it bruised and sore, hasn't it?"

"Yes." The moment I affirm his raunchy allegations, he trails a finger through my arousal, drags it upward, and shoves it into my ass. He syncs the strokes of his dick and his finger, and I rock back to meet him every time, my body granting him an all-access pass.

I'm comfortable with everything he's doing, but I mentally brace myself, anticipate a second finger in my ass at any second. He removes the first one instead, threads his arms through mine and hooks his forearms to pulls me up onto my knees with my back pressed against his chest. "Wrap your ankles behind me. I won't let you fall."

This is a new position for me so I'm tentative as I follow his instructions. The angle is precarious at best. My breath catches in my throat when he puts a foot on the ground, and then drags me to the side and off the couch as his other foot meets the floor and he stands, holding me with my shoulders pulled back, my knees bent and splayed open, and my pussy still speared on his dick. My ankles flex against him to hold on as he walks me across the room to the uncovered windows. "Put your feet on the floor. I've got you." As I straighten my legs and bring them forward, he lowers my shoulders so I can stand, but he's still buried to the hilt inside me so leaning forward is my only option. My hands meet the glass and I try to step back but he doesn't yield any space.

"No one can see," he says. "The windows are tinted. We can see them but they can't see us."

"Are you sure?"

"Yes." His beard is soft against my shoulder, and he

nibbles on my neck. "Or I could be lying. Maybe these windows aren't tinted at all." I shudder, and his laugh is deeply sinister, and so goddamn sexy I hate him for it. "You like not knowing, don't you, sweetness? Thinking someone could look up any minute and see your beautiful body, see what I'm doing to you, watch me savagely fuck you, my hands squeezing these perfect tits they'll never get to touch." He pulls his dick out to the tip and then rams back into me, slamming my forearms against the glass and using the weight of his body to pin me there.

I close my eyes and envision the building. These windows are tinted, mirrored. I know they are, but yet . . . he's planted that kernel of doubt and I'm not sure I can trust what I see in my mind. What if they're only tinted on the front side but not back here? That doesn't even make sense, but I'm not sure what to believe right now. I'm shivering and needy, wanting to shrink back—and shockingly, wanting to be seen, too.

Looking down, I spot only a handful of people milling around behind the building, a circle of five, passing a joint, a couple arguing near the bridge, another pair sneaking off toward the trails. No one is looking up at us. He's right, though. I do like not knowing what they would see if they did look, but I still feel the inhibitions of my own modesty like a stranglehold. "I wish I didn't care what was true," I say.

"Then don't. If these windows aren't tinted, you can't change that, and if they are, there's nothing to worry about in the first place. Why not just lean into what feels good and let go of fear and worry?" He starts to fuck me again, slowly, rhythmically. "What would it change if one of those complete strangers looked up and saw us, anyway? Would this suddenly not feel good?" His fingers clamp onto my nipples, pinch and roll. "Your pussy is starting to cream. You like this so much more than you want to admit." With a gentle shove at my hips, he forces me forward a few steps, closing in behind me to plaster the entire front of my body against the glass. He moves my hands above my head so my breasts are smashed against the window, leaving nothing to doubt if there is no tint obscuring the view. The coolness of the glass on my bare skin, contrasting with the comforting warmth of his body, feels decadent, the dueling temperature sensations mimicking my desire to be cloaked versus being fully exposed.

He wedges his hand between my body and the window and begins to stroke my clit. My first instinct is to tense, to be afraid I won't be able to come again, that I'll frustrate him and myself, but his words sink in, urging me to let go of the fear and embrace the pleasure in the moment, let whatever happens happen.

I close my eyes, notice the glass starting to warm under my skin, imagine there is definitely no tint. My orgasm is quick and quiet, but intense enough to squeeze my walls tightly around his dick, and he doesn't wait for my body to settle before he delivers the savagery he's promised. My breath fogs the window with every yelp as he slams me higher and higher up onto my toes. When his orgasm hits, he's pressed so hard against me that privacy is no longer my main concern about this window. I'm cool with him blowing out my spine, but I'm bartering my soul for this glass to hold.

When he relaxes and pulls me back from the window, I'm actually pretty sure my poor spine has been remodeled to resemble the seahorse on my neck, complete with pixelations. The man keeps his word. I have no doubt I have been fucked.

He picks me up again, cradled in his arms, and I could definitely get used to having him carry me around. The marble counter in his private bathroom is cold under the backs of my thighs and my still quivering glutes. Hollis puts his hand under the running water to make sure it's warm, wets a washcloth, and says, "Spread your legs and lean back against the mirror."

I've never had a man clean me after sex. The warm, soft cloth feels good, and his touch is gentle and I don't even care how I look in this position, or this condition. "God, I have never seen a woman look more beautiful than you do right now." I open my eyes to find him staring at me. He is extremely skilled in the art of seduction. So good that I almost believe him. He's smooth, that's all, but I smile in spite of the obvious. What feels good feels good.

I stare back at him and wonder if he knows, if he could possibly have any idea how important fucking him—being fucked by him—was for me. I'm not the same woman I was when I got on that elevator with him, but if I say that out loud, he'll think I'm a lunatic. "I'm positive no one has ever made me feel more beautiful."

"Good. I like taking a woman to new heights. But I also want to kick the shit out of every man who's ever been with you and failed to make you feel that way."

Give me a minute, I'll make you a list. But first, I'm going to need your services with that washcloth again.

SIX

LATHER, RINSE, REPEAT

I splash water on my face, and then I lean closer to the mirror and dab a fresh cloth under my eyes to tidy up my smeared mascara. Stepping back to survey the results, I look better than I expected. That afterglow is real. There is no taming the frizzled mess of my post-sex hair, though. I've probably got a hair tie buried in the bottom of my purse.

Hollis is using his private shower—a shower in his office bathroom, like some kind of playboy millionaire—but I declined to join him, a decision I regret as I stand here catching glimpses of his silhouetted body behind the glass that's just starting to fog from the steam. He turns suddenly and wipes the glass with his hand, looks directly into my eyes in the mirror. How? How does he always know when I'm looking at him? The shower door opens. "Get in here."

His tone is commanding, and I turn and walk straight into the steam. I hate being told what to do. I don't stand for being bossed around. But somehow, that isn't what it feels like when he directs me. He orders me to do something but makes it feel like an invitation, a strongly worded invitation that I'm power-less to refuse, apparently.

I haven't put my hair up so there's no way to keep it out of the water, and if it's going to get wet, anyway, I'm definitely washing it with his high-end shampoo. He even has the conditioner. I splurged on this brand once. As the intoxicating scent of it fills the shower while I work it into a lather, I decide I'm buying it again. Tomorrow.

A moan escapes my mouth when he takes over washing my hair. His strong hands massaging my scalp is my new kink. *Lather, rinse, repeat forever.* When I turn to flood the suds down the drain, he takes full advantage of the moment and soaps up my breasts. I don't push him away because this is not an unpleasant feeling either, but I've deflected other hands for doing the same. My back arches further in response to his touch, not shrinking back but giving him wider permission. Whatever caused the extreme sensitivity that has always plagued my nipples seems to have been cured by his hands. And his mouth. I squeeze water from my hair and apply a generous amount of conditioner, slip from his soapy hands, and turn around to offer him my back. A girl's got to get clean on both sides, right?

Hollis doesn't hesitate. Bubbles cascade down my body as steam continues to rise around us, and I am positive this is the best shower I have ever taken. I'm talking award-winning cinematography good. He moves his hand between my legs and the soreness registers immediately. "You okay?" he asks.

"Yeah, just a little tender there." His hand skates back up onto my hip and I turn to face him again.

"I'd apologize," he says. "But it would be insincere."

"No apology needed."

He smiles at me, and I swear he looks like a statue come to life, not a soft spot on him anywhere. Water droplets bead against his skin, break apart, and run through the defined dips in his muscles like chaotic streams. I drop to my knees to finish what I started earlier. He doesn't stop me this time, and when he comes, I let him fill my mouth, and I swallow it all. It occurs to me that we've been reckless in more ways than one, but before I can fully process my concern over that, it dawns on me that we've been up here a while. The picnic ends at six and I have no idea what time it was when we took the elevator to his office, or how long we've been secluded in it. He pulls me to my feet.

"Do you have any idea what time it is?"

"None at all," he says, as if it couldn't possibly matter, but then his face clouds. "Oh, right. You came here with someone who might be looking for you."

"Yeah. Not that I want to leave with him. He probably assumed I left already, anyway."

"Must've been a pretty serious fight."

"Serious enough to lead me up to your office, and to put the final nail in the coffin of a dead relationship."

"And I thought a company picnic would provide a fun day for all."

"Well, if I hadn't seen my naked coworker on his phone —" I stop talking. He doesn't need to hear this. "Yeah, not a fun day for me, but it had nothing to do with the picnic. Or this." I look around the shower like I'm illustrating it with my eyes, like he wouldn't know what I meant by *this*.

"I'm sorry you got hurt. But I guess if he's fucking your coworker, fucking his boss was the ultimate way to up the game, huh?"

I can't tell if he's trying to make light of the situation or if he's angry. "I didn't plan for this to happen."

"Of course not. How could you have?" He shuts off the water and reaches outside the glass for a towel. I assume it's for him but he hands it to me before he steps out to get his own.

When I step out, he asks if I need another towel for my hair. I nod. "I'm sorry. I don't mean to use all your towels."

"You need to break the habit of constantly saying you're sorry for things that don't matter. I offered you the towel. Don't apologize for taking it."

"Have I done something to make you mad? You knew I was here with someone, one of your employees, so why are you acting like—"

"I don't give a damn about him. I appreciate his skills, but I pay him for that. I don't owe him any bro-code bullshit. If he hadn't fucked up, you wouldn't be here right now." His words are coming faster, and if he's not angry, he's at least annoyed. He takes a steadying breath. "I'm not mad at you, but it's frustrating to see you make yourself small and shrink back after I've seen you let your guard down and be bold. I think that's who you really are, but you put on this other persona, this people-pleasing act that's not nearly as attractive. That's all."

"You didn't seem to mind being pleased by me." I scrub at my hair with the towel.

"I didn't mean to offend you." He pulls me close. Trying to resist is pointless. Not to mention I want to let him hold me, to press my face into his chest and pretend my life outside this office isn't in shambles. "You've had a shit day and I don't mean to pile on."

"The whole day wasn't shit." I can't help but smile.

He kisses my forehead, and it's an incredibly sweet gesture, but one that indicates this was definitely a one-time thing. We've had our fun and he's done, ready to send me back to my life so he can resume his, where I definitely don't belong. "I'm glad I met you, Oakley. I'm glad you came up to my office, and I'm never going to be sorry for anything that happened between us."

"That would mean a lot more if you didn't sound so completely disappointed in me."

"You want the truth? I am disappointed." *Fuck, just kick me while I'm down, why don't you?* I step away but he grabs my arm before I can turn my back to him. "I'm extremely disappointed you don't have that Annie Oakley tattoo. Huge letdown, honestly." His eyes brighten and his smile is smirky, but way too attractive for me not to smile back at him.

"The day's not over," I tease, but it's a half-hearted attempt. I'm not really in much of a joking mood right now.

"Get dressed so I can take you to dinner."

I open my mouth to list all the reasons I can't go to dinner with him, but nothing comes. So what if Christian's still here? Do I really want to ride home with him? Fight over something that no longer matters? There's an emptiness in my stomach that confirms that picture on his phone was the last straw. I'm truly done with him. Also, I'm starving. "Yeah, okay." I answer as if he's asked a question, rather than stated a foregone conclusion that we would be going to dinner together.

When I open my purse to fish out the hair tie that I'm hopeful is lurking in a crevice, my phone blinks at me with notifications for missed calls and messages. Five from Christian, then one from my best friend, Nadine, because Christian has called her, three more from Christian, then one from Nadine saying she told him I'm at her place but don't want to talk to him. *I'll lie to that fucker any day of the week but please let me know you're okay!!!!!!* I send a quick reply to assure Nadine I'm fine, thank her, and tell her I'll fill her in later.

My pinky hooks the hair tie and I exhale with relief. *Yes!* I have everything a woman needs to start working through a crisis: a best friend and a hair tie. When Hollis pulls his jeans up over those thighs, a third need surfaces: another clandestine encounter with this man who has put my body through more rigors and rewards in a single afternoon than I've experienced in months. Many, many months.

But today was a one-time deal for both of us. Pure revenge for me. For him? Curiosity, maybe, or boredom, just basic horniness, I might remind him of an ex or look like someone he once knew and never got a chance to fuck . . . who knows with men?

SEVEN

EXTRA PICKLES

The elevator doors open to the lobby, every bit as quiet and abandoned as before, but I see as soon as I step out and look through the windows that the picnic is just starting to wrap up. There's still a small crowd on the lawn, most walking toward the parking garage but some standing and talking in groups.

Hollis leads me outside, and we turn immediately for the garage. His parking spot is on the ground level and I'm grateful to be buckled into his passenger seat before we cross paths with any familiar faces.

As we drive out, I see the bartender I lied to about my drink ticket. He's loading an ice chest into a van, and he looks exhausted. The picnic was no fun for him either. I wonder how they clean the margarita machine and what bar he works at and if anyone else gave him a hard time today and why I can't remember his name and how much Hollis spent on booze alone for this event and if my brain will ever stop spinning again.

Leaving feels like entering a foreign land. Everything beyond Nyx International is exactly the same—same congested freeway, same shopping centers and restaurants, same billboards, but it all looks completely different to me now. Where does my life go from here? I'm single for the first time in almost two years, which is fine. I'm homeless, which is not fine. Guess I'll be crashing on Nadine's couch until I get my own place. I need to go apartment shopping ASAP. Tomorrow is Sunday and I have work again on Monday.

The world stopped for me for a little while today, but it's back in motion and moving fast. "You all right over there?" Hollis's voice interrupts my hectic thoughts.

"I'm fine, just a lot to think about."

"You live together, don't you?"

I nod, my head so full of regret it feels almost too heavy for my neck. "I gave up my apartment and moved into his, so I'm the one who'll be looking for a new place. Which is fine," I add in an attempt to sound less pathetic. "I'll look tomorrow. I can probably afford a better apartment now than the one I left behind, anyway. It'll be fun to start fresh."

His smile is sympathetic and that wrecks me because I know he sees right through me. "Things will look better after you eat."

"You're supposed to at least pretend you believe me."

"I've never been very good at pretending. But I do believe you're going to be just fine once you get things sorted out."

"Thanks. Hearing that actually helps. And food definitely won't hurt."

"It's never hurt me." His smile is enthusiastic now. "What are you in the mood for?"

"Honestly? A burger. A big one."

"Challenge accepted. You're about to eat the best burger of your life."

"How are the onion rings? Because those are a must and I have pretty high standards."

"I think your onion ring expectations will be exceeded."

"You haven't let me down so far."

"Good to know." His laughter is contagious, and I don't know how I've gone from existential dread to flirting and laughing again in a matter of minutes, but there might be something powerfully magical about him. Aside from his thighs.

The parking lot he pulls into leaves a lot to be desired, including pavement. And at the head of this gravel patch sits a building that looks like it won't survive the next storm. I find myself leaning to the left as we walk toward it, trying to figure out if the whole building is slanting downward or if it's just an illusion due to the shutter clinging crookedly to the side of a window, looking like it fell off at some point and someone just tossed back at the building and it stuck. There's barely any paint left on the wooden siding and the hinges on the door appear to be solid rust. They squeak as Hollis pushes it open.

The smell of grease hits me immediately, but it's not old, stale, rancid grease. This is the scent of meat sizzling on a grill and freshly sliced potatoes and battered onions frying. Oh, this is the real deal all right. Instant cure for double-crossed hearts. Or a patch, anyway.

My nose follows the smell of something sweet to find a fudge counter along the wall. Every variety of fudge imaginable sits on trays lined with wax paper. There are shelves of jarred candles and house-made condiments for sale at the far end. This place is straight out of a romance novel. The heroine would work here, passing out fudge samples and waiting tables until a handsome, wealthy man, looking for some simplicity in his life, came in and swept her off her feet.

A pretty brunette with doe eyes steps up the hostess stand and smiles at us. I feel a pang of possessiveness I have no right to. *Back off, Bambi. This hero's with me. At least until he drops me off at Nadine's and this fantasy ends.*

Hollis did not oversell the burgers here. They're perfect in every way, including the freshly baked buns, but I can't finish mine. I leave no onion ring behind though. "I can't believe I've never been here. This place is amazing."

"I can't believe you picked burgers when I would've taken you anywhere."

"That's what you get for letting me choose."

"I'm not complaining, but you surprised me. People rarely do."

"It's been a day full of surprises." I pull the sweet and spicy pickle slice peeking from the remnants of my burger and pop it into my mouth. "Some of them were good."

"Like that pickle?"

"Are you kidding? These pickles are the best thing that happened to me all day." I wink, or my version of it, which involves more facial contortions than could ever be cute.

"Was that a wink or did something bite you?"

"You can bite me." I ball up my napkin and throw it across the table at him but he catches it. "Show off."

"I got lucky."

"Yeah, it's been a pretty good day for getting lucky, too." I attempt another wink, making sure to exaggerate my struggle this time.

"That's hot. You should do that on all your dates."

"Oh, I do."

"So, not a lot of second dates then?"

"Second dates are overrated." I shrug and slide out of the booth. "Do you know where restrooms are?"

He points to a very large sign that says RESTROOMS, one I'm sure I would've seen on my own if I wasn't bleary-eyed and half dizzy over him calling this a date. A date. I'm on a fucking *date* with Hollis Nyx? Why this is more discombobulating that the sordid afternoon we spent together in his office, I have no idea. The man has seen every inch of my naked body but I'm nervous about being on the world's most informal dinner date with him?

I find him waiting by the fudge counter when I return from the bathroom. He's holding something I can't make out until I'm standing right in front of him. "You bought me a jar of their pickles?"

"Who said they're for you?"

"Oh, thank goodness. For a minute there, I was worried you thought I might drop my panties for pickles."

"You're not wearing panties."

I was today years old the first time my pussy clenched at a fudge counter. The pretty hostess clears her throat. I give her a wonky wink as we walk past.

Hollis sets the pickle jar in a cupholder in his console. "I have guestrooms, Oakley. If you need a place to stay—"

"No. That's incredibly generous, but my best friend's couch is ready and waiting for me."

"I hate the thought of you sleeping on a couch when there are perfectly available beds at my house."

"If I go to your house, I won't want to be in a guest bed. And I could use a little best-friend time right now."

"That makes sense. You probably need someone you can talk to tonight, someone who knows you."

I give him directions and he doesn't push the option of staying with him. Being with Nadine is what I need, but part of me is tempted by his offer and wishes he'd ask one more time. I'd turn him down again, of course. Most likely.

He puts his car in park and turns to look at me. "I meant what I said earlier. I don't regret stealing you away from the picnic." A stray piece of hair falls across my face and he gently brushes it aside with the back of his hand. "I'd like to see you again, Oakley."

"I'd like that, too."

"I'll be in touch, but I need to know something first."

"What?"

"Your last name."

"Durant."

He leans in to kiss me, and I meet him more than halfway. If he offered to take me home with him right now, I wouldn't be so insistent on staying here with Nadine, but he doesn't force me to grapple with my decision, just gently ends the kiss and says, "Don't forget your pickles, Oakley Durant."

EIGHT
SHARING IS CARING

Nadine yanks the front door of her duplex open before I even reach for the knob. "Get in here, now!" I stumble as she grabs my wrist and pulls me forward, slamming the door behind us.

She has two glasses of wine waiting on the coffee table with the open bottle standing at the ready for refills. "Spill. I want every detail." We snuggle into opposite ends of the couch, each with one of her oversized, fringed pillows at our back, a fuzzy throw across our lap, and holding a stemless wine glass that says: *You Call it Slurring. I Call it Speaking in Cursive.*

"It's like it was fate that I saw it. He left his phone on a table when we stopped to talk to some people he works with. He realized it like five minutes later but he needed to go to the bathroom, so, of course, I went back to get it for him. The text came in while I was holding the phone."

"I can't believe Christian has been fucking Sugar behind your back."

"Honey."

"Oh, sure, like that makes it better. What the hell were her parents thinking?"

"Who knows, but this isn't really about her."

"She knew he was your boyfriend. He was there when she met us for drinks that night. You've been nothing but nice to her and she does this?"

"But I wasn't supposed to be in a committed relationship with her. It's not like I'm looking forward to seeing her at work on Monday, but Christian is the asshole who cheated on me."

"He's always been an asshole. But let's talk about his boss." She waggles her eyebrows. "Did he live up to his hype?"

"His hype?"

"Hollis Nyx? Are you kidding me? When I was in high school, my mom and my aunt used to drool over him every time the Texans were on our TV. He was way too young for them, obviously. How old is he now?"

"I didn't ask. I'm sure it's online. But I guess you can tell your mom and your aunt yes, he is worthy of whatever hype there was about him."

"You really have no idea what a big deal he was, do you?"

"No. I only know he played for the Texans because Christian used to tell me every time he mentioned the guy when he first got the job."

"You didn't just fuck his boss. You fucked his idol! You are a legend and you don't even know it."

"Christian idolizes a lot of people. You know how easily impressed he is by money and fame."

"Okay, whatever, I don't want to talk about him anymore. Did Hollis show you any secrets moves from his playbook?"

Heat rises on my cheeks and I can't fight the impish smile pulling at the corners of my mouth. "Okay, he did this one thing . . . " I set my wine glass on the coffee table to free my hands for demonstrating. "So, we were on the couch in his office and he was behind me—"

"Doggie style. You can say it. Say it, Oakley."

She's needling me because she knows I hate that phrase. "Anyway, he slid his arms under mine and hooked them to lift me." I'm doing a terrible job trying to convey this maneuver with hand gestures, but I keep going. "And then he told me to wrap my feet behind his hips like this." My interpretive reenactment is not getting any better. "And then he freaking stood up and walked me across the room to the windows without disengaging!"

Nadine's expression confirms I've totally failed at explaining it. "Hold on. I need a visual aid." She runs to her bedroom and comes back with Monk-Monk, her giant pink and purple monkey with dangling arms and legs. Separating the Velcro holding his hands together, and then his feet, she shoves him at me. "Here, demonstrate."

"Okay." I hold Monk-Monk's back to my chest, fling his furry-noodle arms over my shoulders, and grasp his gangly legs at my waist. I have to squat and lean back a little to keep him in position as I walk across the living room, which ends up being more of a waddle and not at all the sexy picture I'm trying to paint here, but I figure she will at least get the concept. When I turn around, Nadine has her phone in front of her face. "I will bury you in your own backyard if you took a picture of me like this!"

"What? I thought you might want to see how you looked fucking a monkey. Monkey style!" She cracks herself up, and falls over. "Besides, I took a video, not a picture." Her laughter has literally knocked her sideways.

I can't believe she made me humiliate Monk-Monk for her entertainment. Turning the poor, helpless monkey around, I let his arms and legs hang freely as I carry him back to the couch and set him in what would be a comfortable position, if he could feel comfort. "Do you want to hear about this or not?"

"Yes, I want to hear everything." She sits up and turns her phone toward me, making me watch the video once before she deletes it. "There. It's gone. So, he walks you in front of the windows. Wait, his dick is still inside you while he does this?"

I nod, biting my bottom lip, watching as her eyes expand. "And then he set my feet on the ground, and I put my hands on the glass . . . and I'm still not sure if those windows were actually tinted or not." I'm laughing now. Hearing myself say it out loud makes it seem even more unbelievable. I actually did that? Me?

"Was the picnic going on below those windows?"

"No, everything was set up out front and his office faces the back of the property, but there were some people down there who could've looked up and seen us."

"I have never been more envious of you than I am right now."

"Then we took a shower together in his private bathroom. And he washed my hair."

Wine spews from her mouth. "Give me a minute. I think I just had an orgasm."

"His thighs are like tree trunks, Nade. Sculpted tree trunks."

"His thighs? That's what impressed you?"

"Nothing about him was disappointing, but those thighs . . . you don't understand. Listen, if I ever text you about *Daddy Thick Thighs*, you'll know who I'm talking about."

"Welp, that's officially his code name now. I would give anything to be a fly on the wall when Christian finds out about this."

"Why would he?"

"You're not going to tell him?"

"I thought I'd want to, but I don't. It's enough that it happened, that I know. Maybe I don't feel enough for him anymore to want to hurt him back. All I want is to get my stuff out of his apartment and move on. It's like somebody flipped a switch inside me."

"Pretty sure somebody's name is Hollis Nyx. And he flipped that switch with his dick."

"Actually, I'm pretty sure he may have done it with his tongue."

"Oh, hell yes!" We high-five and Nadine refills our glasses. "Start this story over. And don't skip any parts this time."

By the time I explain the jar of sweet and spicy pickles sitting next to my purse on her coffee table, we are halfway through a second bottle of wine and have concocted an elaborate plan to break into Christian's place to liberate my belongings if he tries to hold them hostage. He won't. I don't think.

When the second bottle hits the recycling bin, Nadine is trying to convince me I should *accidentally* include Christian in a group text about how I spent my afternoon with his boss. I'm not going to do that, but imagining it does provide a dark sense of satisfaction. Maybe I'm not above wanting a little revenge after all. But I'm a bigger person than that. I think.

NINE

HAPPY ACCIDENTS

It's Sunday but not a fun day, not for me. Not even a pile of tropical-fruit-stuffed French toast topped with candied pecans and powdered sugar can put a carefree smile on my face, but Nadine insisted we do brunch before we head over to the apartment to officially move me out and give Christian back his key. Bottomless mimosas hold no appeal this morning. At least the coffee is strong.

And the waiter is hot and flirty, reminding me I am free to do more than flirt now. It feels strange after nearly two years to think about doing more again with someone new. The memory of how much more I did with Hollis yesterday comes rushing in like a tidal wave. Okay, so it's not an entirely foreign concept, but it still feels strange, although I have no complaints about yesterday in his office or at the burger place . . . A gust of wind threatens to turn every turquoise umbrella on this sunny patio inside out. The mere thought of him causes a disturbance in the atmosphere. That finally puts a smile on my face. "Let's get this over with."

Nadine flags the waiter, makes an embarrassing comment about having syrup on her tits as he takes our cards, and she licks her finger to wipe the stickiness from her skin. To be clear, she is not at all embarrassed by her comment. The waiter grins before he walks away, which makes her happy. I tell myself the better mood she's in when we arrive at the apartment, the better things will be for everyone, because the likelihood of her ripping into Christian is slightly lower if she's riding a buzz of hot waiter flirtation.

I text to say we're on the way and that I'm not interested in talking when I get there. We're coming to get my things and get out.

He responds to ask who I mean by *we*. Oh, please. He knows it's going to be Nadine. I don't reply.

He's not at the apartment when we get there. This is a break I hadn't expected. We have my side of the closet packed into suitcases in no time. Dresser drawers are emptied into trash bags, because I need the few boxes we have for my bathroom and kitchen stuff.

With the last bag loaded in my car, we do a final sweep through the rooms to confirm I've taken everything that's mine. I resist the petty urge to take every lightbulb because I bought them when Christian insisted we make to make the switch to LED. I dump all the coffee pods—purchased on my latest Target run, thank you very much—into a plastic bag. I can see how putting the empty box back in the pantry might also seem petty, but at least he'll be able to discover it in the light. *You're welcome!*

I should've known a complete lack of confrontation was too good to be true. Christian walks in to find me standing in the middle of the kitchen, holding the bag. "I was just leaving."

"Talk to me, Oakley. Let me explain."

Nadine squares her shoulders and takes a step toward him. "Let you explain what, exactly? How Squirrelly sent you that nude by accident? Or are you sticking to that asinine story about your brother?" She places one hand on her chest and the other in the air like she's swearing an oath, and in the most mocking tone, says, "I swear, Your Honor. I've never seen that razor-burned pussy before in my life!"

"Leave it alone, Nade," I warn. "I've got this. Let's go."

"Just like that?" he says. "You don't even care, don't even have any questions?"

"Actually, I do have one." Another petty urge is building, one I'm trying hard to tamp down. "Why did Hollis Nyx stop playing football? Did he get injured?" *Because he sure didn't seem injured to me.* It's getting harder by the second to hold my tongue.

"No. His contract in Houston was up. He was a free agent, and he walked away. Could've kept playing for years, raking it in. He's famous for an interview where he said he'd lived for football since he was thirteen and it was time to explore a new frontier. He meant like, in his life and shit, you know, not like outer space or anything, but sportscasters still quote that line and make fun of him for it. He says he just laughs right along with them. He lives with no regrets. The guy's a genuine badass."

How have I lived in Houston for so long and never heard about any of this man's claims to fame?

"He's a man of conviction," I say. My voice carries a tone of wonder and awe, one I should probably rein in before I let myself get swept away in some stupid fantasy. The petty urge to spill about our afternoon tryst is gone.

"Same thing." Christian shrugs. "We just used different words."

"No. We meant two entirely different things."

"Why'd you ask about Hollis?"

"First, you were upset that I didn't have any questions. Now, you're suspicious because I asked one. You seem a little paranoid. It's not a good look." I walk toward the door without so much as a backward glance. "My key's on the counter."

Nadine smiles at me when we get in the car. "Are you proud of me?" she asks.

"For what?"

"Letting you handle that. Great job, by the way. Planting that seed of mystery about Hollis? Brilliant move."

"First of all, I'm not congratulating you for letting me handle my own business. Second of all, I didn't intentionally plant any seed."

"Fine. Then it was a brilliant accident."

"I'll accept that." *No regrets.* "Ready to help me find an apartment?"

"Are you kidding? I've been ready for months. I was just waiting for you to wake up and leave his sorry ass."

I catch a red light and roll to a stop. Christian sends a text accusing me of stealing the TV remote. He probably carried it into the bathroom and left it there. Again. How dare he accuse me of stealing from him! *I definitely should've taken the lightbulbs.* Nadine turns up the music and confidently belts out the wrong lyrics.

"Nade, you don't happen to have a remote control in your purse right now, do you?"

She points at the windshield. "Green light!"

TEN

REALITY IS ABSURD

"I can't believe rent has gone up so much in two years!" I drop all the apartment brochures I collected from today's viewings into Nadine's kitchen trashcan.

"Why do you think I stay in this outdated duplex? Every year I expect a rent increase but my landlord never goes up on it."

"You were dating the guy who owns this place when you moved in."

"Yeah, but that's been over since before you met Christian. Still no rent increase."

"What am I going to do, Nade? Even if I trade in my car for something with a cheaper payment, I couldn't get it low enough to afford any of the places I looked at today. Why'd I give up my apartment to move in with him?"

My questions are rhetorical. I know what I'm going to do. I'm going to sleep on Nadine's couch while I try to find something within my budget that doesn't require over an hour-long commute each way. And I gave up my apartment because I assumed if things didn't work out, I'd be able to rent another one with no problem. My rent would've gone up there, anyway, just like every other property in the area.

But I gave up everything. I sold every piece of furniture I owned, for crying out loud! This was nothing so special about Christian that should've warranted liquidating my entire life. I'm not dipping into my savings to pay rent every month. No more impetuous, irresponsible decisions. From this day forward, I, Oakley Durant, am a fiscally responsible, independent woman. Who just happens to be sleeping on someone else's couch at the moment.

Nadine clears a drawer in her dresser for me. She says it was full of old t-shirts she never wears anyway, but she moves them to the top of her closet instead of packing them up for donation. Her coats and jackets get moved to her bedroom closet so I can have the closet in the living room. I feel like such a burden already. Her bathroom has a double vanity so there's plenty of space for my stuff without displacing hers. "This is actually good," she says. "I like the whole bathroom being used. Feels less sad and lonely."

"You love living alone."

"True, but it was still kind of depressing to have a whole sink and empty medicine cabinet that never got used." It isn't entirely unused. She moves a few things out of the cabinet for me, even though I tell her I don't need that much space. I'm not going to be here long.

"Well, you're here now, and I'm in the mood for pizza."

My phone lights up at the same moment the doorbell rings. Nadine goes for the pizza while I reach to reject Christian's call. But it isn't him. It's a number I don't recognize; hopefully it's the tiny house development I left a message for earlier. They're in a decent location. And if I don't subscribe to any streaming services, I can almost afford to rent one of their four-hundred-square-foot boxes. "Hello."

"Hi. I thought maybe I should check on you since the last time I saw you, you were being sucked into a house by an invisible force."

"Oh, Nadine's a force all right, but trust me, she is not

invisible." The quipped response leaves my mouth as if it's totally normal for Hollis Nyx to be calling me, but my brain quickly catches up, pumps the brakes and let's my giddy nervousness take the wheel. My very visible force of a best friend is joking with the pizza delivery guy at the front door while I spill water down the front of my shirt because I just totally missed my mouth. I hop up from the couch and pull the wet fabric away from my body, looking to the ceiling fan as if it's going to get the message, pick up speed, and dry me out. "Um, how'd you get my number?" *Way to go, dumbass. Now he probably thinks you didn't want to hear from him.*

"I probably shouldn't admit this, but I snooped in your ex's personnel file. Shhh, don't report me to human resources."

"You asked Christian for my number?" Something flutters wildly in my core and I'm not sure if it's because I'm flattered that he'd go so far just to talk to me again, or if it's the beating wings of exalted vengeance taking flight.

Nadine drops the pizza box on the coffee table and pumps her fist at her side, mouthing *Yes! Yes! Yes!* She laughs like a cartoon villain, lifts a slice, twirls with glee, and takes a bite, letting the cheese stretch out like a ribbon of vindication. It snaps right when Hollis confirms the truth. "Didn't have to go quite that far. I suspected you'd be listed in his emergency contacts."

"Oh, shit. Can you remove me from that?" I laugh and take the slice Nadine is offering. We lift our hands and touch crusts like we're toasting.

"I cannot." His laughter is deep and warm, putting me at ease but igniting all my nerve endings at the same time. I feel the phantom heat of his breath tickle the baby hairs at the back of my neck. I'm certain the tactile memories of him are going to linger for a very long time. It may be the only thing I'm sure of right now. "Am I interrupting your dinner?"

"Oh, sorry. I just took a bite of pizza." *And chewed in your ear like a fucking troglodyte.* I pull the phone away from my mouth and swallow.

"I'm starting to worry about your diet."

"You'd be really worried if you knew what I had for brunch. In my defense, there was fruit. But I only eat junk like this on the weekends."

Nadine snorts and rolls her eyes.

"So, if I were to take you to a restaurant with vegetables on the menu one night this week, you would recognize them?"

"Hey, there were veggies on our burgers. Lettuce, tomatoes, pickles . . ." My eyes land on the jar, and my mouth fills with the taste of them, another sensory memory. And I want to kiss him so badly all of a sudden that I almost miss the breadth of what he's said. He's asking me out. On a date, presumably to eat at an establishment with no fudge counter or snickerdoodles-scented candles on a **BOGO** sale. "Yes, it's safe to assume I would be able to identify vegetables on a menu."

"Good. I hate when I have to explain cauliflower."

"Listen, there is no explanation for cauliflower." Our laughter comingles and it sounds so good mixing and weaving together. Damn, how does he make everything feel so easy?

"How does your Wednesday evening look?"

"My schedule is wide open." *Yeesh.* That came out sounding way more desperate than I intended.

"Can I pick you up at seven?"

"Sure. Or I can meet you somewhere. I don't mind."

"I do. I'll pick you up. It won't hurt my feelings if you bring an overnight bag. I'm happy to drop you at work Thursday morning."

"Then I'd have to get a ride home."

"And if that were to be me, I could have dinner with you two nights in a row."

"A man with a plan."

"I have many, many plans for you, sweetness. I'll see you Wednesday at seven."

"See you then."

Trying not to hyperventilate, I collapse onto the couch and contemplate my pizza slice like it's a complicated equation on a chalkboard. "He asked me to go to dinner with him Wednesday night. And to stay at his place after. And then go to dinner again Thursday night." I hold up my free hand and put a finger down for each of his invitations. "That's a lot. It's too much, too soon, right?"

"The way you're breathing right now, I'd suggest you pack enough for two nights." She puts her hand under mine and guides my pizza to my face. "Eat before you pass out on me."

I take a bite but I can't taste anything—until I conquer the lid on the pickle jar and it opens with a pop of the seal. *Yeah, that's what this pizza needed.* Nadine looks on in disgust, but then she lays a pickle onto her slice and tries it. Her eyes go wide, and she says, "Why have we never done this before?"

We watch rich housewives argue, intermittently reaching for another pickle slice between bites. One of the husbands on screen says something degrading to his wife, and before she can respond, one of the other wives—the one she'd been arguing with five minutes ago—grabs a small ceramic bulldog from a side table and hurls it at his big head. Bam! Perfect contact. "Don't you dare talk to my friend like that!" she yells, as he holds his cheek and stutters in disbelief, left speechless by the consequences of his own actions. They replay the moment half a dozen times before the end of the episode. It gets funnier every time. And these pickles just keep getting tastier.

ELEVEN

THE AUDACITY!

I manage to avoid Honey, aka Squirrely, at work on Monday until late afternoon. Working for J & P Event Planning is a dream job, but being the personal assistant for both Jonna and Pepper is a nightmare sometimes. They hired me when the company was still new, but then it blew up, and now they should really each have their own assistant. Garth came on right after me, the original idea being that he and I would tag-team the job. We soon figured out he's meticulous at times where I'm laid back, prone to combustion in moments where I'd shrug and say "close enough," so he became more the enforcer at showtime, and I continue to handle most of the upfront work. Besides, he loves getting to attend all the events for free and I'd rather be home wearing comfy sweats and no makeup. I go to enough functions to keep myself visible, but I duck out at the first opportunity.

Frankly, Garth and I could use an assistant at this point. When Jonna and Pepper decided to hire someone new a few months ago without our input on the prospects, I trusted them to choose a good fit. Just never imagined I'd have to worry about her being a good fit for my boyfriend's dick. Garth spent less than five minutes with Honey on her first day before he messaged me to say she wasn't going to cut it. I became her champion on the spot. Goddess knows, I love an underdog. Just never imagined she'd get under my boyfriend.

Okay, enough. Stop this shit right now. It's not like you can tell Jonna and Pepper you can't work with this girl because she's sucking off your ex. Buck up and be a professional.

"Hey, Honey." I approach her as she looks through the samples I've stacked on the work table, fanning the piles as she goes. We operate out of a small warehouse space in an industrial park. There is no physical office in the traditional sense, no front desk or reception area because there's no room. Every square inch is needed for the showroom. Our phones, computers, and these shelves and tables in the corner are all we need to get the job done. "Did you confirm delivery with the florist for the party at The Parasol tomorrow night?"

"I sent Kay a text on Friday." She yawns and continues to scatter my samples.

"We don't text vendors to confirm scheduling. Did I ever once tell you to text someone during training? We email them so we all have access to the paper trail. If Garth is onsite at the venue for setup, he can't see texts on your phone, Honey. But he can access the scheduling doc to confirm if changes were authorized and when the customer was notified, and he can pull up the email exchanges if he needs proof. He's in the hotseat when he's face-to-face like that. Sometimes clients forget a change was made, and he has to show them to calm them down. People get high-strung and anxious when they're in charge of the details on their end, and they don't always remember everything that happened along the way. Garth is disarmingly charming but if he needs backup to mitigate a situation, it needs to be immediately accessible." My voice is rising despite my efforts to stay calm here, but holy shit, who does she even think she is to be texting a vendor? "We double and triple check everything. And we document it! That's why we have such a stellar reputation of delivering exactly what we promise. Screenshot your text messages to support Kay's confirmation we are on schedule with the flowers exactly as ordered and send it to the J & P email address."

"Send it how?"

"It doesn't matter. In the body of the email, as an attachment, whatever, just make sure you send it so we all have access to it. That's protocol. Always."

"But email it from where?"

"Um, your personal email account? Do you not have the app on your phone?"

"I don't use email. It's basically obsolete."

"Not here, it isn't." I point sharply. "Go sit at that desk and sign yourself up for a free email account, and then figure it the fuck out! It's not hard."

"You know there are software programs we could use for this, right? I don't know why this company can't use current systems. And that's not a desk. It's just a card table and some folding chairs." She sneers at it, and then at me. "It's actually sort of demeaning that I'm expected to work from there."

"It was enough of a desk to launch this entire company! That table and those chairs are how J & P Events started. In Jonna and Pepper's guest bedroom. If it was good enough for them, it's good enough. And if good old-fashioned email is good enough for Garth and me, it's what we're going to keep using!"

"Fine. I just know there are easier ways."

"Just because something's easier doesn't make it better. Save the texting for personal pics. And don't send those to our vendors either. Or to any of their boyfriends, if you can help yourself." I stare at her, knowing I should not have said any of what just flew out of my mouth, but here we are.

She stares back in horror. Her expression betrays bona fide shock.

Does she really not know what happened at the picnic? He didn't tell her? Knowing she would have to face me today? Fucking coward.

Honey quietly takes a seat and starts tapping away on her phone screen. At least she's occupied. I reorganize my previously grouped samples on the long work table.

The rest of us have a late night tonight going over design schemes and swag ideas for a fall trade-show event. It seems far away but we'll need to place orders soon.

My phone buzzes with an incoming group text from Jonna. She's included Pepper. Apparently, Honey wasn't signing herself up for an email account as her fingers were flying. She was texting the owners of the company about the hostile work environment I have created by yelling and cussing at her. I take a steadying breath, tell myself to keep this professional. I'd give anything to be able to tell them exactly what I found out at the Nyx International company picnic on Saturday, and how I found out. But that has nothing to do with my job here, and would probably look exactly like me being hostile.

Me: *She texted Kay Conroy to confirm delivery for tomorrow night's event instead of using email. I told her not to text vendors and to send that text convo to the company email account so we have a record of it. She said she doesn't use email because it's obsolete. And then she complained about not having a real desk and said it's beneath her standards to work from a card table.*

Pepper: *THE FUCK? FIRE HER ASS RIGHT NOW!*

I laugh and wait for the confirmation that she was joking. The bouncing dots tell me someone is typing. When the message displays, it's not Pepper's confirmation of a joke.

Jonna: *I concur. She's done. Fire her ass.*

Wait. What? They can't be serious. I can't fire anyone. That's their job. And I definitely can't fire this girl! She'll sue for sure, saying I did it out of spite. Shit, now I have no choice but to tell them everything. This is not a conversation meant for text messages so I ask if we can discuss some extenuating circumstances face-to-face this evening.

The little dots bounce. They stop bouncing. They reappear. They disappear. Finally, Jonna says yes, we can talk when they get here. And then Pepper follows.

Pepper: *Please tell me you have not been sleeping with this girl!*

A string of laughing emojis scroll as Jonna reacts and then Pepper fires back with more. There is a running joke about me being the only straight person in the company, which has led to some hilarious commentary between the four of us. But I have a bad feeling it may not be funny anymore after I tell them who is sleeping with Honey. How is it that Christian cheats and I'm the one who ends up potentially implicated in a wrongful termination lawsuit?

I look over to see Honey typing away on her phone again. "Hey!" I shout to get her attention. "Text me the screenshot of those messages."

The stunned look on her face is priceless. "The ones between you and Kay. About the flowers for tomorrow night. I'll take care of adding them to an email."

And because my lesser angels are vindictive little twats who own me right now, I add, "Aloe is really good for razor burn, by the way."

I busy myself pulling samples and bookmarking sites to prepare for our meeting tonight and ignore Honey completely until she clocks out. Garth arrives at the showroom before Jonna and Pepper, so it's a full-on family convo when I fill them in on Honey and Christian.

The first reaction of all three of them is that she definitely needs to be fired. I love them for that, but I don't want the company exposed to any legal problems because of my personal life. Pepper promises to run it by their lawyer but she and Jonna both insist they hired Honey with an acknowledged probationary period so they can fire her without repercussions. Not to mention, she used a client's phone number in an unauthorized manner and didn't follow office procedures.

This is where an employee handbook would be useful, but I don't have time to write one so I don't mention it. In a small company like this one, the person who identifies a need is tasked with filling it.

Garth says Honey's lucky he wasn't the one who was told to fire her because he wouldn't have hesitated. It occurs to me Garth might actually enjoy writing an employee handbook.

We order Thai food and focus on the task at hand, putting the Honey issue on a back burner.

Before we close up, Pepper asks if we can reconvene Wednesday evening to finalize the details we didn't get to tonight. When I say I have a date, they all block the doorway and tell me I'm not going anywhere until I fill them in.

"How'd you meet someone already?" Garth asks. "Is it someone from your past? A second-chance romance?"

"Please tell me it's Christian's dad," Pepper says. "Or his brother."

"Or his best friend," Jonna offers. "That could be good, too."

I laugh, and self-consciously tug at a section of my hair. "Um, how about his boss? Hollis Nyx?"

A pyramid of high-fives goes up over my head amidst a chorus of approval:

"Yesssss!" "Nice!" "Damn, girl!"

Garth clutches his chest and says, "That man's thighs are unbelievable."

"That's what I said! But I don't think Nadine gets it."

"Sneak a picture," he says. "You know, for Nadine. But if it was on your phone anyway, and your favorite coworker just happened to see it, who would it hurt?"

"An accidentally seen picture is how this whole mess started."

"No," Jonna says. "It was started by your unfaithful boyfriend."

"That's right," Pepper agrees. "The picture just told you what you needed to know."

"Exactly," Garth chimes in. "And I need to know how big

that man's thighs are in real life so set a quarter on one for scale before you snap the pic."

We laugh all the way to our cars, but I won't be sneaking any pics of Hollis's thighs, or any other part of him. Garth will have to rely on the internet. I'm sure there are plenty of images of Hollis's legs online.

Maybe I'll check later. For a friend.

TWELVE
SHOTS FIRED

As soon as I see Jonna's text Tuesday morning saying I should hold off on coming in for a while, I know they're firing Honey. Nadine breaks into a happy dance, but I feel weirdly conflicted. It's not like I necessarily wanted to keep working with her. And to be honest, she wasn't a good fit for the job to begin with, but I can't shake the feeling that it's my fault.

When a second text arrives with a list of five venues and scheduled meeting times that fill most of my day, it's apparent my employers plan to keep me too busy to dwell on any personal stuff today. I've been asking to take on more responsibility for months, which was one of the reasons Honey was hired, but this feels so sudden now that it's here. And possibly unwise if she's being fired. I know this means someone else will have to take care of the things I was supposed to have done today before these appointments got shifted to me, and now I feel guilty for that, too.

Notifications start pinging on my phone as my calendar updates with the meetings Jonna is assigning to me. She's looking out for me, but she's also trusting me. I've never been the sole face of J & P Events; I've been the tag-along assistant so often I definitely know the drill, but today it's going to be all on me. This is what I've wanted. It's time to put on the heels and deal.

"Shit. I don't have anything to wear and there's not enough time to buy anything before my first meeting. I've gotten so used to working in the showroom, my entire wardrobe is leggings!"

"That's not true," Nadine says, shaking her head and laughing softly in that reassuring way of hers, the one that indicates she's already solved the problem. "You own other clothes. But shop in my closet. Go crazy."

There's something empowering about wearing a new outfit, even if it's just new to me. By the time I hit the road in Nadine's clothes, I feel invincible. The sun is shining and the air feels charged with possibility. I pick up my coffee in the drive-through, adjust my sunglasses in the rearview mirror, and charge the freeway on-ramp like a woman on a mission. This is my day, my fresh start, and I am so ready.

My first meeting is at a remodeled vintage motel aiming to rebrand as boutique lodging and event hosting. They have a courtyard with fountains, some old oak trees that provide a good shade canopy and sturdy branches for hanging lights. There's not a lot of space to work with but it would be good for intimate events. No indoor option for a plan B if the weather goes to shit though, and it would be a pain to get a tent set up under these trees, not impossible, but tricky. I take pictures and make notes.

Next up is a remodeled Victorian home. Now, this is a flexible property. Huge backyard, a nice large room on the first floor thanks to some removed walls. They've wrecked the architectural authenticity of the era, but for commercial purposes, they've created a gem. Limited parking is the only drawback, but we can work around that with a shuttle service. I'm excited to tell the team about this one. I can't resist sending a few snaps of the unexpected size of the indoor space to our group text.

I'm rolling with nothing but positive vibes when I arrive at the rundown dancehall. I recheck the address to make sure I'm at the right place. Maybe he wants us to view it pre-renovation so he can wow us when it's done? I tell myself the interior work is probably done and they just haven't rehabbed the exterior yet. The man who greets me at the entrance has the type of bushy mustache my mom calls a porn-star-stache. *If this guy's done any porn, I hope I never accidentally see it.* I extend my hand and introduce myself.

He replies, "Harold. I don't shake hands with women, and you look like the sort who'd sue me if I tried to hug you, so let's just get to business." *Houston, we have an asshole.*

One step inside the place and I know I've judged it too kindly. It reeks of decades of cigarette smoke and mildew. It's nothing but a shell. Old wood floors, bare walls, no windows, a long bar with no equipment behind it, not even a sink, open ductwork running through the ceiling but it's not new and shiny. Nothing is new or shiny. "What kind of events are you hoping to host here?"

"Long as they can pay, I don't care what people do in here."

I don't doubt him for a minute. "How long have you owned the property?"

"Just bought it. How much you s'pose I can rent it out for?"

The photos I'm taking aren't to pitch the place; they're to substantiate the horror story I'm going to tell about it. "I'm going to be honest with you. I wouldn't have the first clue what someone might pay to use this space. Our clientele is probably not the best market for it, but thanks for taking the time to show it to me." *Ten minutes completely wasted, not to mention the drive time and gas.*

"I guess my realtor was mistaken when she said y'all were a big deal promotion company then."

"We're one of several in the city. I hope you find a better fit. Enjoy the rest of your day." He can't shake a woman's hand but he's happy to ogle my ass as I walk away. I wouldn't have looked back and caught him staring if not for the diamond-back slithering at the edge of his parking lot. "You've got a rattlesnake over there. You might want to get rid of it if you're going to have people coming and going from the property."

"Nah, city girl. Ain't nothing but a rat snake."

"I promise you I know the difference, and that's a rattler."

He laughs. No, scoffs is a better word for what he does.

Harold has definitely put a damper on my productive, happy morning, but I'm not going to let one jackass ruin my day. My phone lights up as I slide behind the wheel. It's Christian. If I had any self-control at all right now, I'd let it go to voicemail, but ignoring two jackasses back-to-back is beyond my capabilities. "Hey, what's up?"

"Seriously, Oakley? You got her fired? Do you know what an insecure bitch you look like right now? Your jealousy is out of control. You need to get help."

"She got herself fired. And she's got you making a fool of yourself. Calm down. Have some juice. Eat a snack. Take a nap. I hear those things can help when children get cranky."

"And which one of us is behaving like a child here?"

"I'm sorry. Did I not speak clearly enough? You, Christian. You are acting like a child." A blast reverberates up from the pavement and through my car like lightning has struck beneath it. I duck behind the dash and drop my phone. *What the hell?*

With my heart hammering in my chest, I peek up to see Harold smiling at me through the windshield. Holding a pistol. "Hot damn, darlin'! You were right! That really was a sidewinder! Got him!"

I can hear Christian yelling my name. I grab my phone from the floorboard and drop it two more times trying to get it back up to my face. "I'm fine."

"That sounded like a gunshot."

"That's because it was a gunshot."

"Where are you?"

"I'm doing my job. And you should probably get back to yours." I disconnect the call and put my car in reverse. Harold waves as I drive away—with his shooting hand, just waving a pistol over his head like a madman. What a day. It's not even noon.

My afternoon appointments didn't have to try hard to outshine the low bar set by Harold's empty, crime-scene-in-waiting snake pit. This day has been full of adrenalin rushes and crashes, and I can feel my energy draining as I input the venues I saw today into our database. Well, four out of the five get input, anyway.

Pepper comes into the showroom practically bouncing on her toes. "You sure charmed the heck out of Harold." She carefully sets an elaborate rainbow chandelier she's just had custom-painted onto the floor, leaning it against a portable bar. That light will be Instagram famous in no time. "How was his place? I couldn't get a clear visual from the way he described it."

"Did you envision a dump? Because that's what it is. And he fired a gun in the parking lot as I was leaving."

She pulls up a chair. "Start at your arrival and walk me all the way to the gunfire." I give her the whole story, from him refusing to shake my hand to waving goodbye with a gun. "Okay, you win for wildest venue viewing ever. Wow. Jonna's going to shit when she hears this. The guy acted like it went great, like he expects we'll be booking events there right and left, said he's looking forward to working with us."

"You know how in the movies when someone is being tortured for information or because they're a snitch, it's always in an old, empty building in the middle of nowhere? Well, if we get a call from anybody looking to duct tape a guy to a chair and peel his face off, Harold's got the perfect spot."

"Put that exact comment in the notes, please." She laughs.

"You really want me to add that place to our venue list?"

"In this business, you just never know. Put it in."

"Whatever you say. Does it even have a name? The only sign said dance hall and that was it."

"Use that if you want, or you can just put in Harold's name. I don't think we'll forget who he is anytime soon."

"Harold's Rattlesnake Saloon it is."

"Perfect. You're done for the day. Go home."

"I'm already gone. You can't even see me anymore." I pause and look at the chandelier again. "They did a really good job on that."

"Right? I dropped off two more this size to be painted the same way, and two smaller ones to be done in a pink ombré. And I've got a huge one with a guy who's going to dip it in chrome for me. That's going to look sick with disco balls around it."

"You are the funky chandelier queen."

"That's my secret stage name."

"Nothing about you is a secret, Pepper."

"As far as you know. Go. Relax. Boss's orders."

I follow Pepper's orders from the moment I walk in the door. Nadine gets all the details of my day—including Christian's crybaby call and Harold's rattlesnake kill—over dinner, which consists of grilled cheese sandwiches and popcorn with extra butter, striking the exact ratio of carbs to grease that my body needs right now.

Right before I drift off to sleep, Hollis sends a text: *I hope you had a good day. I'm looking forward to tomorrow night.* I hear the words spoken in his voice. Some people might feel weird about jilling off on their best friend's couch, but I'm never going to be able to fall asleep if I don't. It's not like I'm going to call Hollis and ask him to talk me through it. That would be so inappropriate.

Well, if he knew what I was doing, but if he had no idea, then no harm, no foul, right? I reply to his text: *I'm still up. You feel like talking?*

My phone rings in a matter of seconds. "Hi," I say, barely above a whisper so my voice doesn't carry down the hall to Nadine. Not that it would be heard over her noise app and her fan, but better safe than embarrassed.

"Hi. How was your day?" He is not whispering, and his deep voice is exactly what I need to hear.

"It was wild. Remind me to tell you about it tomorrow."

"Why not tell me now?"

"I'd rather hear about yours. I wanted to hear your voice before I fell asleep." I slip my hand inside my sleep shorts and stroke my soft skin, letting two fingers skate through my wetness.

"Why did you want to hear my voice?"

"I like your voice. It's soothing."

"You need to be soothed, huh?" Why does he sound amused by that? "Is there anything in particular you want me to say?"

"What? No. Why?" *Fuck. I think he knows.* I yank my hand out of my shorts like a kid caught in the cookie jar.

"Do you need me to help you fall asleep, Oakley?"

Say yes. Just tell him. You're a grown woman. He'll probably be into it. Probably won't think you're a complete weirdo at all.

"You there, sweetness?"

"I'm here."

"All alone on the couch?"

"Yes."

"Is your pussy warm under your hand?"

I slip my hand back inside my shorts. "Yes." My voice is barely audible.

"Are you wet enough to slide two fingers inside?"

"Yeah."

"Mmmmm, God I wish I was the one touching you right now." My seahorse tingles when he says, "Pinch your nipple with your other hand. Is it hard?"

"Yeah." My responses have become more breath than words.

"Drag your slick fingers up over your clit. Close your eyes and circle it. Can you feel my mouth on you, my tongue massaging you there? Oh, fuck, you taste so damn good. Where are we, baby?" I know he doesn't need answers to his questions anymore. He's prompting me, and it's working. We are in the courtyard of the motel I saw this morning, under the oaks, me lying on a table while he works me with his mouth like he did when I was on his desk. The sound of the fountains is eclipsed by the noises he's making. All the rooms face the courtyard and anyone could see us so easily, just like the people below could have when we were at the window in his office, but closer. Someone could walk right up on us out here. "That's a good girl. Roll your hips for me. Show me where you want me, how you like it. I love how juicy and sweet your pussy is right now. Do you need fingers inside again? Give yourself what you need. Keep one hand on that swollen clit though. Pinch it between your fingers. Squeeze it, make it feel like it does when I suck on it. Yeah, there you go. Show me how rough you want me to get." He swallows and his mouth sounds wet and warm. The memory of his face looking up at me from between my legs causes my breath to hitch. "I can't get enough of you when you're needy and eager, shoving that sopping wet snatch in my face, riding my mouth like a perfectly shameless little whore. My sexy little slut who can't get enough of having her pussy licked while her tight creamy cunt clamps down on my fingers, showing me how good it's going to feel when I ram my hard cock inside and make you scream my name again."

And that pulls the pin right out of the grenade. I bury my face in a throw pillow and come harder than I ever could've imagined from phone sex. I can't believe we just did that. And I'm nowhere near ready to analyze the fact that I rocketed to orgasm after he talked to me like that. Since when I am into *that*? And how did he know when I didn't even know?

"Do you think you'll be able to sleep now?"

"Pretty sure I'm going to sleep like a baby." *As soon as my pulse stops racing.*

"Good. If you made anything sore, ice it. Because tomorrow night, it's all mine. Sweet dreams."

"You, too." I press my phone to my chest and sink lower into the cushions. I've only known this man for three days and I feel closer to him than the man I lived with for nearly two years. I can't tell if my life is spinning out of control, or if I'm gaining control of it for the first time.

BUTTERSWEET KISSES

It's been a good day: no snakes, no gunshots, no accusatory phone calls. And I have a hot date tonight. I still have no idea what I'm wearing but I've never been so excited to pack a suitcase. To not even be going on a trip, no less!

Nadine breezes through the front door with a plastic department store bag slung over her shoulder. A couple hangers poke out the top of the bag, and it's tied in a knot at the bottom. She drops her purse onto the couch next to my packing stacks. "Oh, good. You're not dressed for your date yet." Tearing the bag open, she says, "What do you think?" She's holds up two black dresses, and quickly moves one to her other hand so I can see them both.

"They're both cute, but I like that one better." I point to her right hand.

"Of course, you do. The halter style is for me. You always go for the plunging neckline with the thin straps. I know you. And I knew as soon as I saw it that it was the perfect little black dress for you. And then I realized I didn't have one. So, now we both do!"

"You bought me a dress? Why?"

"So you'd have something new and sexy to wear to dinner tonight. Work was slow. I took a long lunch."

"I freaking love you. How much was it?"

"Doesn't matter. It's a gift."

"You're already letting me stay here for free."

"And now, I'm gifting you the perfect little black dress because I am the perfect best friend." She swishes the dress back and forth as she hands it to me. "But you can't hog the bathroom to get ready because I have a date tonight, too."

I feel a little better knowing she went shopping for herself to begin with and my dress is a byproduct of the trip. "I need five minutes to finish packing, and then the fight for the mirror is on."

The dress fits like a glove, but all I can think about is Hollis taking it off.

It feels like the butterflies in my stomach are playing hide-and-seek. They settle for a few minutes, and then suddenly flit around frenetically again, as if they've been found and are scattering for a new hiding place.

He's punctual. I knew he would be. Nadine makes me spin in my dress so she can do a final inspection before I walk out the door. "Like sin dipped in sugar. Go blow his mind. See you tomorrow night."

"I hope you have the best date of your life tonight, Nade." I hug her before I open the door to find Hollis wearing black on black—the tie, the shirt, the suit. *Like sin. Dipped in sin.*

I introduce him to Nadine, and he says it's a pleasure to meet her, adds that he's heard so much about her. "Oh, I've heard an awful lot about you as well." Her tone makes it clear she's heard everything about him, and his smile indicates he already suspected she had—one part cocky, a million parts sexy.

When he pulls to the curb in front of the valet stand, and I realize where we're having dinner, I'm even more grateful to

Nadine for bringing home this dress. A man rushes to open my door and help me out of the car. There are large, gas-lamp sconces on either side of the entrance to the restaurant, and through the front windows I can see the modern lighting sparkling over the bar. Christian and I had reservations here once, for my birthday. I made them. He canceled them, saying instead of spending so much money on a meal and drinks, he'd cook for us at home and buy me something that would last. Our dinner ended up being frozen salmon that he over-cooked and mac and cheese from a box. My gift was a pair of small, silver hoop earrings almost identical to a pair I already owned and wore all the time. Wonder where he got the wildly original idea I might like silver hoops that size. I was so disap-pointed at the time, but now all I can think is how glad I am to have no memories of this place with Christian so I can experi-ence it for the first time with Hollis.

"I hope this is okay," he says when he catches me staring at the lights beyond the glass.

"It's great."

A svelte woman in a black jumpsuit and strappy heels leads us past the bar area to the dining room. Her hair is upswept and I'm sure the giant diamond studs on her ears are real. She's dressed as nice as the customers. Hollis orders a bottle of wine by name. It's something French. Or maybe Ital-ian. When he asked my preference, all I said was red. And then he opened his mouth and some beautiful sounding words flowed out and the waiter complimented his choice. *I said red, like it was a distinct choice.*

When I open my menu, it's all I can do not to choke on the tiny numbers printed in a hard-to-read fancy font next to each item. I know these prices aren't shocking to him, but I wish the wine would hit the table already because I could use a little liquid shock absorber.

He proposes a toast after our wine is poured. "To new

beginnings. I'm very much looking forward to getting to know you, Oakley."

I can't find adequate words to respond, and saying *same* seems on par with having said *red*, so I simply smile and touch my glass to his. This is such a *date* date. It's hard to believe the sophisticated man sitting across from me is the same one who bought me a jar of pickles. He's comfortable anywhere. I'm not sure if that makes him a down-to-earth good guy, or a chameleon con-man I should be wary of. Apparently, cheap earrings weren't the only things Christian gave me. *Thanks for the trust issues, asshole.*

My salmon is perfectly cooked and Hollis's wine selection is excellent. It doesn't take long before I'm every bit as comfortable sitting across from him here as I was in the burger dive. Before I know it, he's asking if he can twist my arm into having dessert, and I'm telling him the truth: "I never don't want dessert. I've had to talk myself out of it, but never into it. But, let's split something."

I love his laugh and the way his piercing eyes narrow and create tiny lines at the outside corners. The waiter brings the dessert list and goes over each one. My mouth waters when he says, "Butterscotch pot de crème." Butterscotch is my absolute favorite, but I'm convinced it's the least popular flavor in the world. No one ever shares my enthusiasm for it, and the options in front of me include all the popular choices: choco-late cake, cheesecake, bread pudding with bourbon sauce. . .

"Close your eyes and look away," I say.

He raises his eyebrows. "Why do I have to do both? That seems like overkill."

I raise my brows in retaliation. "You told me to choose. And I like to surprise people."

"So far, you've been excellent in the surprise category." He winks before closing his eyes and turning his head to the side. I point to my choice and the waiter nods and mouths, *it's so good.*

Hollis is deep into teaching me what exactly a defensive end does on the football field when our dessert arrives. He's so serious about it. His focus on explaining what the player has to be aware of and prepared for is impressive. He clearly loves the game, but I can see what he loves most. It's not just the strategy, but the sudden twists, the need to think and act quickly that gets his heart pumping. It excites him to have to be on his toes, ready for the unpredictable. The small white dish being set down between us stops him short, even before the waiter speaks. "How did you do that?" he asks, pointing at it and staring at me like I just turned a football into pudding.

"Do what?"

"How did you know butterscotch is my favorite?"

"Are you teasing me because you hate it?"

"I'm being amazed by you because I love it. I just didn't expect you to pick that."

"I don't seem like a butterscotch girl?"

"Definitely assumed you were a cheesecake girl. But once again, you've surprised me."

"If it makes you feel better, cheesecake was my second choice."

"If only they'd had butterscotch cheesecake," he says, teasingly.

"I might've made sounds that would've gotten us kicked out of here."

He laughter rolls out like a bass line as he feeds me the first bite, and I have never had such erotic thoughts about a dessert before. For the rest of my life, the taste of butterscotch is going to be a portal right back to this moment.

The night air has an unusual chill for late spring. Hollis removes his jacket and drapes it over my shoulders while we wait for the valet to bring the car around.

We've only driven a few blocks when he suddenly whips into a parking lot.

Before I can ask what's up, he releases his seatbelt and leans over the console. His beard tickles my cheek while his husky voice does the same to my eardrum. "I can't wait any longer for that butterscotch kiss." I adore that tone, the way it somehow abrades and assuages at once.

His mouth is warm and sweet and buttery, and oh, damn, I'm glad he pulled over for this. If we weren't parked under a light, I'd give him much more than a kiss. As if he can read my dirty thoughts, he breaks our kiss and flashes a pirate smile, his eyes glittering with devious intentions. "That hot mouth is the only thing sweeter than your pussy." His hand slides up my thigh until he meets the satin and lace of my thong. "You wore panties tonight?"

"I do that sometimes."

"Take them off." The command floods my tastebuds with butterscotch. And I'm pretty sure I've flooded my panties, but I remove them for him. As soon as I've slipped them over my shoes, his hand is out to retrieve them. He glances at the glistening slickness in the center, smiles wider, and then tosses them into the backseat. His hand climbs back up my leg. People walk past on their way to whatever club or restaurant they're destined for, paying us no mind at all. This is a pay lot. We can't stay here for long. His fingers stroke me a few times before he plunges inside to coax more of my juices onto his skin. Instead of pressing his fingers inside my mouth to have me suck them clean, he traces my mouth, coats my lips with my arousal, and kisses me again, licking and biting aggressively, but I'm matching his verve. He stops seconds before I'm about to invade his lap. "Mmmm, best flavor combination ever, sweetness."

No other man has ever talked so much about the taste of my pussy, and if they had, I'm positive it would've made me want to spin myself into a cocoon, but when Hollis so openly expresses how much he enjoys it, all I want to do is stop, drop, and spread eagle.

He refastens his seatbelt, puts the car in drive, and pulls out of the lot, leaving me breathless and agitated. If not for the raging hard-on bulging at the crotch of his black pants, I might be upset at the way he teased me back there. But we're both in a bad way, and I already know my first night in his bed is going to be more memorable than any dessert.

FOURTEEN

THINGS I SHOULDN'T SAY
(TIMES A MILLION)

I didn't expect Hollis to live in a modest home by any means, but I had envisioned him in something more modern. His house is large but it's . . . homey? It's nothing like the streamlined design I imagined. After seeing his office, this probably shouldn't be such a surprise. Polished wood floors, large, comfy looking furniture, rock fireplace, and original paintings on the walls, depicting recognizable subjects—nothing abstract in sight. Everything has a what-you-see-is-what-you-get vibe.

His electronics aren't even hidden in sleek cabinets. There is a giant TV mounted on the wall but it's not hidden by any fancy panel. It looks like he has enough stereo equipment to start a sound studio, but it's all visible. To be fair, any amount of stereo equipment seems like a lot compared to the one Bluetooth speaker I use to listen to music from my phone.

This place isn't something the average family could afford, I get that, but it's also not a showplace meant to impress; it's a home, his soft place to land after a hard day, and it's filled with his favorite things. I spot the turntable, and it makes me laugh. "You have a ridiculous vinyl collection, don't you?"

"When you say ridiculous, are you prejudging my taste in music or the number of records I may or may not own?"

"Way to answer my question without answering my question. You own a million and they're all terrible."

"I own slightly less than a million, and they are all fantastic." He kicks off his shoes and leaves them where they land while he slides open the long cabinet under the TV. Oh, yeah, he owns a million, and I know without getting close enough to read the covers that they're in alphabetical order. He tips a record out of its sleeve and spins it between his hands. "Do you know who Elton John is?"

"Of course, I know who Elton John is. Tiny Dancer? Duh, I've seen Almost Famous a million times."

"Do you have any benchmark for a large quantity other than a million?"

"No need." I shrug. "A million gets the point across effectively."

The strain of his jaw as he tries not to smile does at least a million different things to me, all of them fantastic. "Take off your shoes. Make yourself at home." He nods toward the couch, and my mind immediately casts images of us on the couch in his office. "Let me introduce you to a wider selection of Sir Elton John." After he sets up the record, he turns to me and says, "I'm going to open a bottle of wine. I assume you want red?"

My cheeks heat, but I laugh. "Good guess."

Before he goes to get the wine, he loosens his tie, pulls it free, and drops it onto a chair. He untucks his shirt, undoes the top few buttons, and unbuttons the cuffs. The music begins to play, and his tattoos slowly come into view as he meticulously rolls a sleeve upward. It's a forearm striptease, and I'm mesmerized. I pull my feet up under me and lean back into a soft pillow.

When he has his sleeves the way he wants them—and me melting into a languid mass of submissive putty—he turns and crosses the room toward the kitchen, his footsteps muted by raucous piano notes. His broad shoulders tapering down to his taut torso creates one hell of a hot silhouette as he walks away.

If my panties weren't still on his backseat, they'd be a complete mess by now. Without the material against me to contain it, I can feel the slickness seeping out as I shift on his couch, no friction, only the smooth glide of skin on skin. Sweet surrender, I would let this man do anything he wanted to me right now. There is a salacious little fairy on my shoulder dying to force those words right out of my mouth. I'm about to drown her in red wine—or give her the strength to take over completely. It can be tricky to predict the effect of a third glass of wine on a tiny orgiastic fairy, especially one with a horny phrase already tap dancing on the tip of her tongue. Not to mention I haven't felt her presence in quite a while, so there is actually no telling what she might make me do before the sun comes up.

I don't think Hollis needs me to tell him how compliant I'm willing to be right now, though. Pretty sure his dick has psychic abilities. The man has surreptitious ways, and I am enraptured.

His wine is as smooth as the one we enjoyed with dinner. And his kisses taste even sweeter with the ruby vintage layered onto his butterscotch tongue. Our exuberance from the car has been tempered, but this is nice. Long, slow kisses that are still scorching, but there's no hurry. We've got all night. Literally.

I am about to spend the whole night with him, wake up next to him with morning breath and bed head . . . and if there is a higher power at all, his hard cock pressed against my ass, announcing his need to fuck me once more before we leave this oasis and go back to our regular lives. I can't remember the last time I woke up feeling needed like that, and the prospect is electric, but what I'm feeling right now with his breath rolling like thunder while he kisses me is more than a long-forgotten sensation—this is new, unlike anything I've felt with anyone before him. Everything with him feels like a first, but with the benefit of experience.

He pulls me onto his lap and rucks my dress up around my hips as I straddle him. Elton sings about cartoon balloons and a porch swing while Hollis lifts my dress off my body and sends it sailing. The only light in the room comes from a lamp in the corner, and the glow softens our edges until we blend where we touch. His hands gently glide up my sides to trace the curve of my waist, keep going until his huge palms conceal my breasts. He caresses, doesn't grope. My nipples knot, and he pulls his hands back until his fingers alone maintain contact.

I make the mistake of glancing down to see my nipples between his fingertips, which immediately turns up their sensitivity. He increases the pressure of his squeezing. He's testing me, watching to see how much I can take, and I want to endure so much more for him, but I need something else to focus on, a distraction so my eyes will stop signaling my brain to retreat. I kiss him again, and it is absolutely the right call.

Being completely naked on his lap while he is still fully clothed should probably make me feel vulnerable, but it does the opposite. I feel powerful and sexy, and his kiss is getting hungrier, more aggressive. Because of me. For me. His hands leave my tits to roam back down my body. He squeezes my ass until I'm lifting off his lap, and in an instant our kiss has ended and I'm face down on his lap, just like I was on the couch in his office.

I've gone from powerful to conquered—no, that isn't true. Not conquered, I've surrendered. I let him flip me into this position with no resistance, and my whole body is quivering as he rubs and squeezes my cheeks. The anticipation of the first slap has me squirming over his legs. His hand smacks my ass, and the sting clings to my skin. In the few seconds before he strikes again, my shoulders relax and my nerves stop tap dancing. There is no fight or flight, only acquiescence. But I acquiesce as much for my need to feel this as for his desire to do it.

"God, I love the way my handprint looks on your gorgeous ass."

When he'd said that to me for first time in his office, I'd been shocked by the words, but now I'm basking in them. My body's innate reaction carries no shock at all this time. His dirty dominance has my pussy clenching air and craving something far more solid to constrict around. My thighs are slick and I love they way they slide against each other with every spank that makes me shift on his lap. It's instinct to move away from pain, but my body denies it more with each contact.

Hollis's hand rubs over the heat he's created on my ass, and then he moves between my legs to explore the fire he's stoked there. His fingertips dance along my seam for a few minutes, or maybe only seconds exaggerated by his teasing until they feel so much longer, before he slides two fingers inside and twists them back and forth. The side of his hand presses against my inner thigh, nudging me to open my legs wider for him. He spreads my juices everywhere, and I try not to tense up, feeling sure his finger is going to enter my ass when he traces me there, but he flips me over instead.

He pulls me up until I'm almost sitting, holds me cradled in his left arm while his right hand continues to probe. "Spread your legs completely. Butterfly them open for me." I let my knees fall to the sides like he's asked as he plunges his fingers deeper into me, maintaining eye contact as he does it. "You like having your pretty little pussy played with like this, don't you?" I think I nod but I know the word that's audible in my head doesn't actually leave my mouth. His eyes are like magnets attached to mine, and I don't think I could break our gaze if I tried.

"Why can't you tell me?" he asks. My shrug is slight, but again, no words. I'm splayed open on his lap and what he's doing feels lewd beyond measure. And good, so damn good. I don't have access to the words to tell him, though. They exist. I can feel them when they form, even hear them in my head, but there is a roadblock somewhere between the place where the words come together and where my voice infuses them. He isn't upset with me, just genuinely curious. I think he's a man who likes a good challenge, and maybe I'm becoming one. Not because it took any convincing for me to have sex with him, but he wants me to talk, to say what I like and what I want, and I'm more comfortable letting my body carry on that conversation. He understands my body language, but he wants me to cross the barrier holding back my vocal assertions. I've never been able to get there. But the difference is I want to with him, whereas before, it never mattered to me.

"Squeeze my fingers, show me how tight you can make it." I lock down the necessary muscles and he smiles. "Mmmm, yessss. So fucking perfect." His eyes leave mine long enough to scan my naked body at his mercy. "Every inch of you is perfection." Sex talk, and I appreciate it, but my body is far from perfect: stretch marks on my hips from weight fluctuations in my teens, that weird section at the top of my inner thighs that won't firm up no matter what I do, the way one nipple is slightly larger and lower than the other . . . I know it is what it is, and no body is truly perfect, but being inspected this closely, there's no way he hasn't noticed these imperfections on mine. "Don't do that," he says, his eyes locking back on mine. I raise my eyebrows questioningly. "You tensed up and pulled away when I said you were perfect."

I didn't feel that happen, not outwardly, anyway. Damn, he may be too perceptive with body language.

A smile is all I have to offer. His smile in return tells me we're good. He pushes his fingers deeper and begins to stroke upward.

My eyes drift closed and my head falls back when the base of his hand starts to grind over my clit. *How is a hand that big so deft? Maybe he should've been the guy who caught the ball instead of the one who knocked the other guys down.* I've definitely never thought of football during anything sexual before. I laugh a little and bring my head to rest on his shoulder. "If this tickles, I must be doing it wrong," he whispers, playfully.

"You are definitely not doing it wrong."

He keeps doing it until I'm panting in his lap and setting tiny shrieks free against his shoulder. His fingers still but he doesn't remove them. As soon as my breathing subsides, he starts again, gentler to begin with. "You're going to come for me again before I carry you to my room."

When he mentions carrying me, it jettisons me right back to him carrying me into his private bathroom, setting me on the counter, and everything that followed. My second orgasm comes quicker than the first and leaves my body feeling spent, but nothing could make me not want whatever he has planned once we enter his bedroom. *Or whatever spontaneously occurs.*

His room is large and filled with big furniture. Big enough for him. He sets me on the edge of the bed. I lean back until my elbows find the mattress, and I watch him undress. There is no performance aspect to it, just the mechanics of removing his clothes, but I'm here for the unveiling of those thighs. I wonder if there could ever come a time when I'm not astonished by them. It's not tonight, that's for sure.

Stepping to reach me, he pushes my legs apart and starts to drop to his knees. I sit up. "No, I've already had two—"

"And you're going to have three, four, maybe more. As many as I want you to have. Lie back."

Yes, sir. I almost say the words aloud. Words I've never almost said to any man in my life, but something inside me wanted to say them—like, really wanted to say them. Would he like that? I think he might, but I don't think I could ever actually do it. It's just not me.

He's taking his time, kissing his way up my calf, his beard prickling my skin, his firm hand massaging its way up behind his mouth. Skills for days. Every flick of his tongue, every change in pressure or angle is exquisite, but I can't get the words I almost said out of my head. I imagine what it would feel like to say it, to be that reverential.

When I see it through in my mind, I know he likes it by the way his eyes flash in surprise, followed quickly by the gleam of victory. And my body is providing proof in real time of how much I like it, churning it out faster than he can consume it.

My clit is captured between his teeth for a moment, just long enough to set me on edge before he sucks it with his perfect rhythm. My back arches of its own accord. The bridge of my spine goes higher as the intensity builds, and before I realize it, his name is on my tongue, and then out of my mouth. Multiple times.

That smile. So proud of himself as he looks up at me. I'm proud, too—of what, I'm not exactly sure. Maybe because I feel like I put that smile on his face? The push-pull vibe between us is satisfying in a way I can't describe. The me-you-us of it all is overwhelming, the way it comes on so suddenly and feels so right. But it's too soon for this to be anything more than physical; not that I'm complaining about the physical. There could be more, but more takes time. All I know for sure is that I was right before: he is the most gorgeous man I've ever seen—between my legs or anywhere else.

Climbing onto the bed, he presses the length of his body next to mine, caresses my cheek, and then my jaw. And then he shoves a thumb into my mouth, grasping my jaw as he does it. I let my tongue trace the bend of his knuckle, noting how rough his skin feels as I map the ridges. The heat in his eyes could incinerate the walls around us when I begin to suck. He pulls his thumb away and kisses me, forcing me to taste my arousal on his tongue, but there is still a hint of butterscotch and wine. He kisses his way down my neck, sparking a shiver when he reaches my chest. Feeling his tongue move across my nipple and not wanting to recoil from it is such a strange sensation. My body still tenses momentarily, expecting the heightened and uncomfortable sensitivity that used to hold court there, but the level of sensitivity residing there now provides a feeling I not only tolerate, but could possibly grow to crave. His touch is transformative, both his hands and his mouth.

When he rises up and brings his body over mine, the width of him blocks the spinning blades of his ceiling fan, leaving only the tips of shadows strobing beyond the sides of his shoulders. I practically float under his kisses until he tells me to turn over. His hand slides between my legs, making me wonder why since he absolutely knows how wet I am. But when he drags his finger to coat it fully, I know exactly where it's headed next. One of his fingers is the size of two of mine but it feels like more when it breaches my ass and presses onward, stretching and filling me.

I gasp when his cock glides into my pussy. My tightness provides minimal resistance with all the natural lubrication still prevalent, but having both holes filled is gasp-worthy, nonetheless. He groans and begins to pump his finger in time with the slow thrusting of his dick, which has the circumference of about seven of his huge fingers bound together. Approximately, but fingers feel like an accurate unit of measurement in the moment. His pace increases, along with his approximate girth. The swelling is almost painful, but in the most divine way possible. I feel him twitch and I twitch in response, like some sort of erotic Morse code, but it's all involuntary.

And then I soak the comforter beneath us. Also involuntarily. I did not feel that coming. Okay, I guess technically I felt it but I had no fucking idea *that* was what I was feeling. It was so subtle. Until it wasn't. Hollis nibbles on my shoulder as if he isn't shocked in the least about what he's elicited from my body. I guess women squirt for him all the time. Talented bastard. I'm drawn back into reality as he extracts his finger from my ass.

Every crude physical necessity feels somehow less Pornhub, more Hulu Original with him. Not to yuck on the former, but I'd rather star in the latter. If he could hear my thoughts, he'd probably call me an Uber. Or a therapist.

He blows on my ear to get my attention. "You in there?"

"Yeah, I'm right here."

"If I ever do something you don't like, you'll tell me, right?"

"I will. You didn't do anything wrong."

"You could also tell me if I do something right."

"Um, I think I did?"

"With words, Oakley."

"I know what you meant. I'll work on it."

"We'll work on it together. I want you to feel comfortable with me. There is nothing you could say that would be wrong."

You might want to hold that thought.

FIFTEEN

GRANTING WISHES

I'm disoriented when I first wake up. It's dark and I'm not on Nadine's couch. These sheets are soft and the mattress feels like a cloud. The moonlight shining in through the giant windows casts just enough light for me to make out his profile when I roll over. Hollis. In the middle of the night. Strong jaw, Roman nose, massive shoulders. His ridiculously unfair eyelashes flutter when he senses me looking at him. I slip out of bed before his eyes are fully open and walk as softly as I can to the bathroom, which isn't so soft. I'm stompy by nature, especially when I'm not fully awake.

The light in his bathroom automatically comes on when I walk into the room. I shut the door as quickly and quietly as possible, which isn't so quiet. I guess I'm a little slammy by nature, too. In my defense, the sudden brightness startled me and I'm temporarily blinded. I stumble to the toilet. My mouth tastes like stale wine, and other things that aren't off-putting in the moment but you don't really want to taste again hours later. But my toothbrush is in my bag, which is still on the other side of the door. After I wash my hands, I squeeze some of his toothpaste onto my finger and give my teeth a quick once-over. It's better than nothing.

Hollis is groggy, but awake enough to pull me against him when I return to his bed. He makes an excellent big spoon, but I usually prefer that spot. I'll let it go for now, but if this sharing a bed thing becomes a habit, I'll have to break it to him eventually. He turns my face toward his and kisses me. Sweet, sleepy kisses. "I used my finger," I say.

"What?"

"To brush my teeth. I didn't want you to think I used your toothbrush. I used my finger."

"Oh. Well, in that case, I wouldn't recommend using it for anything else for a while." His large hand is back between my legs again. "Might be a little tingly. All that peppermint could be hazardous to delicate areas." He's nuzzles my neck, and his middle finger is already circling my clit. And I can guarantee any tingling I feel is not peppermint-induced.

"'I'm sorry I woke you up, but I don't think I can have another orgasm. We should go back to sleep."

"I think you can. And I can't go back to sleep until you do."

The guy's insatiable. But for my orgasms. Is that even a thing? If I let him get me off again, I'll have to return the favor. I weigh the costs, and sink into him. I come with my ass squirming against his hard dick and his finger working my clit like he's winding thread back onto a spool—in a timed contest. He rolls over onto his back as soon as I'm done, and I shift to my side and start to slide down him. "You don't need to do that," he says. "I promise, it'll be there in the morning." His heavy arm wraps me up, and before I know it, I'm drifting to sleep with my head on his chest, but he miraculously beats me to dreamland. Unless this whole night has been a dream, which feels like a very real possibility.

When I wake up for the second time in his bed, it isn't his sounding alarm that gets my attention. It's his massive thigh that I've got my leg flung over as if he's my man-sized body pillow. My eyes aren't even open yet but I'm mentally envisioning his Herculean leg under mine. He carefully abandons the bed for the bathroom, trying not to disturb me. I listen for the shower to start, but the door opens and I know he's coming back to me. *Yes, bring that back, please. Oh, yeah. I owe him an orgasm. At least I can crawl between his thighs to do it this time.*

I do exactly that when his back meets the mattress again, and he doesn't stop me this time. My hands roam up and down his thighs, traversing his quads like I'm drawing my life's energy from them. It's not like I need my hands to get his erection into my mouth—it's standing as rigid as a marble obelisk.

He fires quickly but I'm sure he could've prolonged it if we didn't both have work. "Shower together?" I ask. *Who said that? I hate sharing the shower when I have somewhere to be.*

"If we get in the shower together, neither one of us is making it to work on time. It's all yours."

Apparently, I'm not the only one who prefers to shower alone in the mornings. Checkmark in the plus column for sure. Although I wouldn't be opposed to having him wash my hair again.

I step out of the shower to the smell of breakfast. No way. *Fucks like he does, is kind and funny, and cooks? Nope. I'm calling the government to report an alien walking among us.*

My ovaries somersault as I watch him pull croissants out of the oven, bare-chested, wearing nothing but a pair of low-slung pajama pants with the drawstring untied. "Did you make those?"

"Yes. Well, technically, they came frozen in a bag but I put them in the oven."

A smile overtakes my whole face. "Okay, good. At least I know you're real."

"I'm not sure I want you to explain that."

"No, it's probably better if I don't."

"Hope you're good with ham and cheese."

"Big risk. What if I was a vegetarian?"

"I watched you devour a cheeseburger the day we met. And it was real beef, not the fake stuff."

"Okay, but what if I didn't eat pork?"

He points to a bunch of bananas. "I would never let you go hungry."

"I like that about you."

"And I like that you actually eat," he says as he takes a bite. I grab a croissant and a paper towel and head back down the hall. "Where are you going with that?"

"I'm taking it to go so I can finish getting ready."

"What if I don't allow food in my bedroom?"

"I guess you'll have to make an exception."

"Or punish you later."

What's wrong with now? Another silent reply that I half wish I had said out loud. I didn't hold it back because of the time and our need to get to work; it just hit the usual roadblock. I shrug and take my forbidden flaky breakfast to his room.

The ride to work feels too short. Was there traffic? Did he stop at red lights? I remember getting into his car and the goodbye kiss. And now I'm alone with a long to-do list and my swarming thoughts. I text Nadine to see how her date went. Her response is uncharacteristically enthusiastic.

Nadine: *How mad will you be if I make you wear a yellow dress as my maid of honor?*

Me: *You don't want a husband. You just want the honeymoon.*

Nadine: *The audacity!*

Me: *The accuracy.*

Nadine: *True. Are you still smitten with Daddy Thick Thighs?*

Me: *Do not mention his thighs. I'm trying to work here.*

Nadine: *Be ready to tell me everything when you get home tonight. I'll have Monk-Monk ready.*

Me: *Listen, I can't even look that monkey in the eye anymore.*

Garth breezes into the showroom smelling like an herb garden.

"New cologne?"

"The whole line. Body wash, lotion, cologne. Can you guess the scent?" He waves his arm in front of my face.

"I'm picking up notes of green."

"What a nose. You've truly missed your calling. The top notes are an herbal combination. Basil, sage, and rosemary, with a base of sandalwood and ylang ylang."

"Nailed it."

"Yes. Perfumers the world over should be clamoring to hire you." He starts coffee brewing. "So, let me see it."

"See what?"

"The thigh pic."

"Ha. Ha. No thigh pic."

"Rude. Well, at least tell me how your date went."

"It was nice."

"Oh, I'm sorry."

We laugh, and then I tell him a little more. Garth is one of those people who won't let you get away with the highlight reel, so I give him a few extra details while keeping it as vague as possible. I leave out the spanking, make mention of his strong dirty talk game, leave out my newfound tolerance of nipple play, but make a general comment about Hollis' other oral skills. When Garth's curiosity is finally sated, he hugs me and says, "Girl, you deserve this so much. From sleeping with a loser to a super star. This is your Cinderella-level sexual awakening story. And I love to see it."

I'm taken aback. Garth never said anything bad about Christian while I was dating him. To find out so abruptly he thought the guy was a loser all along is a shock. Unless, he never thought that until the cheating came to light. That's probably it. "Thank you. Your ardent support of my sex life is appreciated."

"I'm here for you. But I'm also out of here because I've

got an appointment with a wedding planner who wants to sub out some events to us. I swear, she is an absolute tyrant. There should be a word for that, like bridezilla but for the wedding planner instead." He pours hot coffee into an insulated tumbler and screws the lid on tight. "Think on it and let me know what you come up with."

"Sure, since I've got nothing else on my mind today."

"Get your mind out of the gutter and get to work."

I'm blowing through my emails and whittling down my list when Christian calls. Not a text. I am so not in the mood for him to ruin my day. I send it to voicemail. He calls right back. Fine.

"Hey," I say.

"Hey. I just wanted to let you know you left something here. I'll be around tonight if you want to come get it."

"What is it?"

"Something you might need now."

"Pretty sure I took everything I needed. Whatever it is, you can toss it."

"I don't know. Seems like you might want this."

"I'm busy, Christian. What is it?"

"Something blue. From the nightstand."

Oh, right. That. "I took the toys I wanted."

"But you left the one I bought you just to be a bitch."

And now we know the real reason for the call. "No, I did not leave it to be a bitch. I left it because I don't want it."

"Well, what am I supposed to do with it?"

"Honestly, I don't give a hot goddamn flying mother-fucking rat's ass what you do with it! Go crazy. Knock yourself out!"

"I hate to see you becoming bitter, Oakley. That shit ages people. Not to mention, hardened women aren't desirable. I really want the best for you. My hope is that you'll be able to move on someday and be happy."

"Yeah? Well, I'm no genie but I can grant that wish.

Consider it done. I've moved on. I'm happy. And I have no need for an enormous, blue, silicone cock. I'm partial to the real deal these days."

"Trying to make me jealous by pretending you're seeing someone new isn't going to work, babe. I'm trying to be honest and real with you, but you're clearly not ready to communicate like adults."

"Oh, go stick your big, blue dick up your ass! Or, have Squirrely do it for you. Whatever works for y'all. Like I said, I'm busy." I end the call. I had no intention of letting him know I had already been with someone else, and I still don't need him to know who it is, but the rush of satisfaction that he knows I'm not sitting around, mourning the loss of him in my life is invigorating. My to-do list doesn't look so daunting anymore.

SIXTEEN
SOLO SATURDAY

Nadine's date went so well she goes out with the same guy on Thursday and Friday, and she stays at his place both nights, which is nice because she tells me to sleep in her bed when she's gone instead of on the couch, but not so nice because I don't have anyone to talk to or eat dinner with or watch trash TV with.

She came home to do laundry and go apartment hunting with me today, but it's Saturday night and here I am, all alone again, and still with no viable prospects for a new place to live.

Hollis is busy with work. He's sent the random text here and there but no calls. It's not like we're dating. He doesn't need to plan his weekend around me, but I can't lie, I was hoping he'd want to see me tonight, maybe invite me over.

Nade's bed is too small for two, too lonely for one.

This is a bad sign. I shouldn't be thinking about him so much. The man has a full life. My life isn't empty: fun job that I love . . . but what else? Before Christian, I used to do things. Yoga. I could do that again. I *should* do that again. Reading. I used to read all the time. Why'd I stop? Weekends trips. Do I want to do that alone, though? Not like I can afford to go anywhere before I find a place to live, anyway.

It's still nice to fantasize about taking a trip, whether I can go now or not.

The problem is it's not a girls' trip that comes to mind. If I think of the beach, I see Hollis half-naked on the sand, holding my hand, walking at the water's edge. If it's somewhere that requires a flight? Hollis is with me in the airport bar. Tucked away in a mountain cabin? Yeah, no way I'm there without him. A rebound guy is supposed to be someone you can't picture in your future. I can definitely picture Hollis beyond the present. And I definitely need to stop.

But is it so wrong? Maybe at twenty-six, a rebound guy isn't necessary.

Is a rebound person really psychologically required to get over someone, or do we just enjoy the thrill of diving into bed with someone new, and the easier means of dealing with the pain?

That's not what it was with Hollis. Except, maybe it was? I was looking to get even. No, I was looking to get ahead in the hurt-me-hurt-you game. That's not even who I am. It was a spur-of-the-moment decision.

A rebound move by definition. *Fuck.*

But I've resorted to a rebound guy in the past and it was clear what was happening. This feels unclear in every way. The lust isn't confusing at all. But the constant thinking about him makes me feel like I'm a teenager again, hormonally obsessing over a guy, who probably isn't thinking about me nearly as much. He's older, established, already on his second career while I'm still trying to get my first off the ground. He's made millions, and I'm searching farther from my desired area of town every day in the hope of finding a one-bedroom apartment I can comfortably afford.

I have no right to expect anything from him, or to feel slighted in any way. Hell, I'm the one who started this whole thing, and I sure didn't pursue him with any pure intentions. He knows exactly why I flirted with him. I wanted to use him.

Although, he is the one who admitted he'd been "eye fuck-ing" me. Right off the bat. He just came right out and said that when we were complete strangers!

I could just as easily come right out and tell him I want to see him. Yeah, no. Nothing easy about that. Maybe if we hadn't started the way we did, but if I ask to see him, it will sound like I'm reaching out because I want to have sex again. Which I do. So, why do I care? I've reached out to guys before. He's no different. Except he is. Dammit! He wasn't supposed to be different. He wasn't supposed to make me stupid.

I silently promise Monk-Monk there will be no defiling as I drag him in for a hug in Nadine's bed.

SEVENTEEN

THE BITCH IS BACK

I promised myself I wouldn't whine at brunch about things cooling off between me and Hollis, and it's an easy promise to keep because Nadine has barely given me a chance to speak at all. She's dicknotized like I've never seen her before. You'd think she custom-ordered Mr. Perfect from a catalogue.

"I feel like I should meet this guy."

"If you're home tonight, you can meet him when he picks me up for dinner."

"You're seeing him again tonight? That's five nights in a row, Nade."

"And I'm not sick of him yet. This may be a record. When are you seeing Hollis again?"

"No idea." I stick my knife into my champagne flute to spear the strawberry trapped in the bottom. The waiter appears tableside to offer me a fresh mimosa, as he whisks the empty glass out of my reach. "He's still texting, but he hasn't asked me out again. Maybe I did something weird."

"What would you have done that was weird?"

"Um, hello, this is me we're talking about. I'm an agent of

chaos, and he's a master of Zen. How's that supposed to work?"

"Yin. Yang. Perfect balance. He's probably just been busy."

"Yeah, maybe. Or maybe getting croissant flakes on his rug was too much. He probably has ants now and he curses me every time he squishes one." I drag the same bite of pancake through syrup for the millionth time. "Or maybe I'm too inhibited for him."

Nadine chokes on her French toast, saves herself with a bubbly glug. "Monk-Monk would like a word."

"Monk-Monk and I are good. We've bonded since you've been gone so much lately. I may file for custody when I move out." I raise my glass. "Which will hopefully be soon. Here's to successful apartment hunting today."

"Today's your day." She taps her glass to mine. "But you know you can stay with me forever. Grow old on my couch. Steal all my monkeys. It's fine."

~

"What do you think? Is it too weird to live in someone's backyard?" I open and close a kitchen cabinet in the converted three-bay garage, now a literal garage apartment.

"This place is so damn cute if you don't take it, I might. If the owner travels as much as she says, you'll hardly ever see her. It'll be like you own the place, but live in your garage instead of your house, like some kind of eccentric artist."

"There's so much more space than I expected. And I had no idea it would have an actual separate bedroom. I thought it would just be one wide-open room. This is bigger than any of the apartments I've looked at. No stairs. No sharing walls with neighbors. It comes with a washer and dryer. I keep thinking there has to be a catch."

"The only downsides I can see are no pool and no gym.

But the privacy more than makes up for that. I think you better jump if you want it."

"You're right. Welcome to my new place."

Nadine wraps me in a tight hug. "I am so freaking happy for you." She releases me and inhales like she's smelling freshly-baked cookies instead of fresh paint. "This is where your life gets really good. I can feel it."

I sign the lease, agree to water Marlise's plants once a week when she's away, and generally keep an eye on the house for her. It's all done. An hour ago, I was ready to give up and accept that my only option was to respond to an ad and move in with a stranger. Now, I have a landlord instead of a roommate. Her name is Marlise and I live in her renovated garage. It's all shiny and new. And I want to text Hollis to tell him about it so badly my fingers ache. *Dammit.*

"Text the man, Oakley."

"What?"

"Tell him you found a place. His response could tell you everything you need to know. Maybe he'll offer to help you move."

"I sold all my furniture when I moved in with Christian. Why did you let me do that, by the way?"

"I'm clearly a terrible friend. Let's go furniture shopping. You need a bed. Then you can tell Hollis you got a new place and a new bed. His response to that will definitely tell you everything you need to know."

"All I can afford is a frame and a mattress."

"That's a bed. You'll put a cute comforter on it. And I'll buy you some throw pillows as a house warming gift. Before you know it, this place will be fully decorated. But let's start with the bed, for multiple reasons."

"I should've taken all the decorations I bought for Christian's place."

"Nope. You're starting over here with all new stuff and a whole new outlook."

Yeah, a whole new outlook. I should've at least taken my candles, though. Christian hated my candles, probably threw them all in the dumpster. Asshole. Now I'm mad at him all over again.

~

There is nothing fun about mattress shopping. It's boring and they're all overpriced, but when I finally decide on one, they say they can deliver it on Tuesday, which is sooner than I expected. It feels surreal to think that three days from now, I can wake up in my brand-new bed in my own place.

Okay, how could I not text Hollis with that update? I want to shout it to the world.

Nadine is driving so I'm holding my phone when his response comes through. Short and sweet: *Congratulations!*

That's it? I guess Nade was right. It tells me everything I need to know. My hand buzzes with another incoming text: *Can I take you to dinner Tuesday night to celebrate?*

Much better. I accept. And then I make the announcement about my apartment in our group text for work. Jonna, Pepper, and Garth all respond immediately. Jonna says taking Tuesday off is no problem. Pepper tells me how thrilled she is for me. Garth offers me a side table he bought at an estate sale yesterday. He says it doesn't really work in his space, but I suspect he may have bought for me to begin with.

"I need candles."

"Of course, you need candles," Nadine agrees. "And pillows. And rugs. Do you have wine glasses?"

"Nope. Adding them to the list of immediate needs."

With my red shopping cart already overflowing, I know I should head to the register. This haul is going to knock a dent in my bank account. But I can't help myself.

"A record player?" Nadine weighs the validity of this choice. "Do you even own any records?"

"No, but they sell those here, too."

"New Oakley listens to vinyl, huh?"

"She's full of surprises."

"Oh, she's a goddamn delight so far. I can't wait to see what kind of music she listens to."

"The same kind she always has." *Plus Elton John.*

EIGHTEEN

A BORN STORYTELLER

I flop onto my bed as soon as the delivery guys leave. Before I even put the sheets on, I starfish, and then I roll around to choose my side. With that decided, I position Garth's gift in the right spot. It makes the perfect bedside table. Next to my perfect bed. In my perfect apartment.

There is no one to weigh in with an opposing opinion on my coral sheets or floral comforter. The appropriate number of decorative pillows is at my sole discretion. Fringe everywhere, pillows, rugs, even on the throw I fold across the foot of the bed, purely for decoration. I stand back and admire the final results. Cue the deep sigh of satisfaction. I'd forgotten how great it felt to have the only say in everything in my home.

A couple secondhand barstools caught my attention online yesterday, and they were still available when I got off work, so I took it as a sign they were meant for me. I have a place to sit while I eat and a place to sleep. It will be a work in progress for a while, but it's livable and it's all mine. I have sumptuous towels, scented candles, cute wine glasses, and a dinner date. Two weeks ago, I was living an entirely different life.

As I stand in my kitchen and look around my completely

undecorated living room, I realize Hollis is going to come to the door, and then I'm going to have to invite him in to see my place, and what he's going to see is nothing but open space.

And a record player on the end of the bar. He's totally going to know I bought that because of him. Mine isn't sleek and expensive looking like his black and silver turntable. It's turquoise and made to look like a vintage suitcase. Cute as hell and it plays fine. Maybe I should at least hide the Elton John album. That might escalate imitation from flattery to stalker mode. But I've listened to it all the way through half a dozen times. Both sides. I like it.

Hollis' headlights stream in through my blinds as he pulls up the driveway. My stomach flinches when his car door closes. *Wait. Who is he talking to?* I peek out. *What the hell is happening?*

He is hugging Marlise. Holy shit. They know each other. What if they dated? Has he fucked my landlord? Please, don't let that be true. I think she's quite a bit older than him, not that it has to matter, but I can't see them together. Except I'm seeing them together right now. What if they're currently seeing each other? No. He would've recognized the address, right? What if they're related? I step outside. "You two know each other?"

"Marlise is my attorney." He throws his hands up. "I wasn't holding out on you, I swear. If I'd known she had this apartment, I would've told you about it."

"If I'd known you were dating this guy, I'd have never let you move in." She and Hollis laugh like old friends, who've probably never seen each other naked. But Marlise is his attorney, which means she knows way more about him that I do. Why does this feel so weird?

Eventually, they're done catching up and it's time to show off my new place. That I'm renting from his friend. Or his attorney with whom he's friendly, anyway. Yeah, still weird.

"Well, this is it." I swing the door wide and step inside,

really wishing I'd put the record player in a closet now. It's so bright against the white quartz countertop and light gray cabinets, like it's screaming *Look at Me!* At least I had the good sense to put Elton John under the sink.

"You're in a great area," he says, looking around at my room full of nothing.

"My bedroom's ready." That sounded different in my head, but it's already out of my mouth so I may as well keep leading him onward. "Here's my only furnished room."

"That is a ridiculous number of pillows. Smells nice, though."

"Thanks. I like candles. And pillows."

"You've gotten a lot done considering you just moved in today. No boxes left to unpack? That's impressive."

"It would be a lot less impressive if you knew how few boxes I had." *Would it have been so hard to just say thank you and leave it at that? He probably thinks I own no worldly possessions at all. I basically don't, but it would be nice if my brain would run a quick check on what I'm about to say before I say it.*

"A fresh start can be a good thing."

"Yeah, that's how it feels."

"Let's go celebrate that feeling." When I try to step past him, he pulls me in close and kisses me. "I couldn't wait any longer to give you your first kiss in your new place. Unless someone beat me to it."

"One of the mattress delivery guys offered, but he was clean shaven." I rub the back of my hand down his cheek. "Guys without beards just don't do it for me anymore."

"Good thing I decided against shaving mine off today."

"Did you really almost shave it?"

"Yeah, but I think I'll keep it for a while now." He tickles my ribs, and I squirm in his arms. "Ticklish. Good to know."

"If you tickle me hard, I will claw your eyes out if that's what it takes to get away from you. You've been warned."

"Sweetness, I don't plan on doing anything to make you

want to get away from me." We kiss again, and this all feels so incredibly familiar and warm, not just like we've kissed in this way before, but like it could've happened right here. "You keep kissing me like that and I'll let my beard grow to my waist for you."

"If you keep it exactly like it is, I'll keep kissing you like that."

"Oh, I see. You want things exactly the way you want them. Short beards, a dozen candles per square foot, a *million* pillows . . . am I getting this right?"

"Precisely."

"I'm taking you to one of my favorite restaurants. Do you like ceviche?"

"Love it."

"You never disappoint."

"I hope this ceviche doesn't disappoint."

"If it doesn't meet your expectations, I'll buy you a pillow factory."

"What? No candles?"

One more kiss and we're headed out the door, which is a testament to how hungry I am because my mattress hasn't even been broken in yet, and his beard really is the perfect length—and not just for kissing.

The restaurant has an entire menu devoted to ceviche combinations. I must be the only person in town who's never heard of this place because it's packed. We sit outside on the patio under fairy lights and misting fans, sipping on palomas and eating ceviche samplers until I forget which one was which. I could never pick a favorite and order it again, and that's fine. I'm enjoying myself too much to keep track of anything other than his stories.

He likes talking about his family, playing football but not

his fame as a result of it, his company but not the ins and outs of what they do, he talks about the people. I'm not a recluse by any measure, but he's a people person, and I'm not exactly that either.

"Do you have any siblings?" I knew questions about my family were coming. Definitely not my favorite subject.

"No," I say. "I'm an only."

"I wouldn't have guessed that. Are you close to your parents?"

"No. I never knew my dad, and my mom's not motherly by nature. She loves me and I love her but she's always kind of had her own life. I wasn't neglected, just not necessarily nurtured. Not her thing. The best way I can describe my upbringing is that I had a guardian who made sure I had everything I needed and a lot of what I wanted, but she assumed I'd get the emotional stuff from friends. It wasn't awful. It just wasn't warm and fuzzy."

He studies my face like he's waiting for me to finish. But that's all there is to say. "Some people would feel resentful about being raised that way."

"I went through some of that as a teenager, but it doesn't change anything. She is who she is. Like I said, she's not a horrible person, she's just not a great mother by traditional standards."

"You ready to order something more substantial?"

"You really want to order more food? After all the ceviche we've eaten?"

"Uh, yeah. Those were appetizers. I want an entrée. You should eat more, too. You might need your strength later." He winks and it's cheesy and hot at the same time, and no one should be able to pull that off.

I order grilled snapper and a side salad. He has the stuffed trout, roasted potatoes, sauteed mushrooms, and a side salad. "I can't imagine how much you ate when you were playing football."

"Much more than this," he says. "One time . . ." And he's off, telling me a story about a team dinner when a truck crashed into the restaurant. It sounds like it's going to be a tragedy, but it ends up being funny, and the amount of food he describes being on their table is mind blowing.

His stories are all big and audacious. That's the way he's lived his life. No fear of failure, just following his passions up with hard work and dedication and believing things will work out the way they're meant to.

I don't get it, but I'm enamored of it. And him.

I'm entirely too old to have a crush, but I swear there's no other word for the way I feel when I'm with him and I watch his eyes dance when he speaks, and the way his mouth quirks when he smiles. When he laughs, it erupts from his core. And even his casual touch makes my skin sizzle. I am a grown-ass woman crushing so hard on this larger-than-life man who shouldn't even know I exist.

But he does, and he wants to know more. It not the thrill of the chase. I never made him chase me. We just sort of fell into each other at the worst possible moment to build anything from, but it feels like something is building here, and I'm pretty sure that's not just the cocktails talking.

NINETEEN

COMPROMISES

We skip dessert but this place doesn't do valet so we're parked down the street, and we have to walk right past a gelato truck. And they have butterscotch. Because fate, obviously. "I've never had butterscotch gelato," I say. "Not sure I've ever even seen it."

"Me either but I'm about see a spoonful of it up close and personal."

The guy inside the truck passes out an over-filled cup of gelato but only one spoon. "Guess we're sharing a spoon," I say.

"Won't be the last thing we share tonight." He scoops some gelato onto our spoon and offers me the first bite. "I hope."

"What's it worth to you?" I tease.

He extends the whole cup toward me. "Here. Take it. It's yours."

"I'm flattered."

"How flattered?"

"Hmmm, I'll show you in about fifteen minutes."

"I bet I can get us back to your place in nine."

"You're willing to run red lights for me? Now I'm really

flattered. I don't know if a guy has ever broken the law to get me naked before."

"What kind of lazy assholes have you been going out with?"

We both freeze for a second, awkwardly suspended in time. "Eh, I wouldn't call him lazy," I say.

"Good to know since he's on my payroll."

I was making a jab at Christian's apparent excess energy for other women. A part of me thinks Hollis knows that, and he intentionally turned the comment in another direction. I laugh and we let the moment pass.

The gelato cup is still almost half full by the time we reach his car but I can't eat another bite. Hollis finishes it off in under three seconds and tosses the cup at a trashcan. He misses. "Good thing you weren't the quarterback," I say. His laughter lingers in his wake as he jogs forward to put the fallen cup where it belongs.

Bringing him back to my apartment doesn't feel as intimidating as showing it to him earlier, but it's impossible to ignore the contrast between his place and mine. Clearly, we can't spend time on my nonexistent couch, listening to music before we move on to the bedroom, but there is no question that he's coming in.

As soon as the front door is closed behind us, his mouth is on mine. I stumble when he tries to walk me toward the bedroom while kissing. He picks me up. I didn't do it intentionally to get him to carry me, but I wouldn't put it past me if it had occurred to me, either. He lowers me to the bed and starts tossing my throw pillows onto the floor. *I gotta get a chair for those. He'll probably still throw them on the floor.*

He unbuttons his shirt, and I watch because I will never get tired of watching him do that. "Why are you still fully clothed?" he asks.

I go up onto my knees and pull my shirt over my head, shimmy out of my skirt, and toss both onto the floor with the pillows. *Definitely need a chair in here.* But I stop there because I like having my bra and panties removed by a man, and this is still new enough that he'll do it. I think. He doesn't hesitate to remove his own underwear.

He's already hard but he wraps his hand around his erection and gives it a few up-downs as he walks toward the bed. Sweet baby Jesus, I could watch that on a loop all day long. "Take off your bra."

Done and headed for the floor.

He stands next to the bed, still slowly jacking his cock and says, "Now the panties."

"Yes, sir." *That was audible. I didn't mean for it to be but he has me in a fucking trance and it just came out. I said it. And not sarcastically. Softly, but obediently.*

His reaction is everything I could have hoped for and more. I only get my panties as far as my knees before he pushes me onto my back and yanks them off the rest of the way. He crawls on top of me and stares into my eyes. "Mmmm, I liked that." He drags his swollen tip through my seam and I lift my hips, trying to entice him to give me more. "Are you going to be a good girl for me all night?"

Oh, hell yes. I bite my bottom lip and nod. "Yes."

"Yes, what?" He pulls his dick away completely.

"Yes, sir."

With a hard thrust, he slams into my pussy until his balls slap my ass. I gasp and squeeze my eyes shut. "Open your eyes, baby girl. Look at me." I had no idea I wanted to be called that but I gush when he says it. Eyes wide open and locked on his with his cock buried inside me, I contract my walls to squeeze him a few times and watch his eyes glaze over.

He maintains eye contact as he fucks me with long, slow, deep strokes. My hips rock up to meet him. This pace, his body so close to mine, the hard thrusts, the intensity of his stare—it's the most intimately filthy sex I've ever experienced, and I never want it to end.

"Tell me what you're thinking right now," he says.

"How good this feels."

"You like my hard cock punishing your sweet pussy?"

I whimper, but it's definitely not a pain response. And nothing about this feels like punishment. He smiles and it's wicked and hot, and I'm not at all self-conscious about the way he's peeling back my layers, discovering things about me as I explore them for the first time myself. Learning me, and teaching me, too.

"You're so sloppy wet. Is that all for me?"

"Yes, sir."

"Is this pussy mine?"

"All yours."

"It's my slutty little cunt and I can use it however I want?"

"Use me."

His kiss is savage, and he can't fuck me hard enough for either one of us right now. We're bucking and thrusting and panting and never breaking eye contact through it all. And then he slows and eases us back to where we began, and this is some form of sweet, addictive torture because I need him to go back to the brutal way it was, but I need it to stay like this just as much and all at once.

This switch is apparently exactly what he needed because his stare releases mine and his focus gets erratic. I squeeze as tightly as I can and then relax in time with his rhythm, milk him again every time he reenters me. His muscles start to twitch, and his jaw tightens. His orgasm racks his body while I watch from below. He collapses on me and I play with his sweat-damp hair, which gives him chills, sending a shiver across his shoulders. "Sorry," I whisper.

He kisses me softly and then rolls off to lie on his back and catch his breath for a few minutes. I like watching him regain his self-control almost as much as I like watching him lose it.

"I'm the one who owes the apology," he says as he gets up and goes to the bathroom. He comes back with a towel. "Sorry I jumped ahead of you tonight, but I needed that worse than you know."

"It's okay if you get yours first. It doesn't always have to be me."

"Yeah, but I like it to be you more often than not."

"It has been. But that was incredible. I'm definitely not complaining." He takes the towel when I'm done, carries it back to the bathroom and drops it on the tile floor instead of my bedroom rug. It's not quite the hamper but he got close.

My now well-broken-in mattress gives under him. He props himself up on his elbow, and I move next to him to lie my back. I could look up at him forever, but he lowers his head to kiss my shoulder, and then his mouth trails down to my chest. His hand cups my pussy as his mouth claims my nipple. I twirl his hair while his thumb circles my clit, and I realize how in tandem we are, and how easily it's happened. I smile and close my eyes, relax into him.

Just like when we were fucking, as soon as I'm wrapped up in the current momentum, he changes things up on me, but this time he goes from slow and smooth to fast and rough. I feel the urgent pressure as he hammers against the magic spot. I've read a million articles on how to hit it and none of them recommended this method.

The viscous release is sneaky and copious as always, and now my comforter has been fully christened. He releases my nipple and pulls his hand from between my legs, smiles at me in that knowing way. "That was worth the wait," I say.

"I love making you do that." His fingers trace my swollen nipple. "But I'm not done. I need to hear you come hard, see you writhe and arch while you ride it out. Do you want me to use my hand again, or do you want my mouth this time?"

"Your mouth?"

"Are you asking me or telling me?"

"Your mouth."

"That's my good girl."

I jerk away from him at first contact. The sensitivity is still too much. He kisses my hipbones and works his way back in, reading my body like a book. By the time I come again, his beard is drenched and we're both spent. "Will you stay?"

"We've both got work tomorrow and I didn't bring anything."

"Yeah, I know." *I was so happy to be all alone in my own place earlier but that was before he got here. I want him to spend the first night with me so badly, but I don't want to be clingy and obnoxious. That's a lie; I want to beg him, but I'll like myself much better tomorrow if I don't.*

"But I am pretty exhausted. I guess I could get up really early and go home to get ready, get out of your way so you can do the same."

"You could."

"Twist my arm." He holds his massive arm up and I pretend I could actually twist it. "Okay, okay, you've convinced me."

I'm so glad he's staying that I don't even mention he's on my side of the bed. I'll break it to him next time. But we do need to get one thing straight. "I like being the big spoon."

"You couldn't be the big spoon if you cloned yourself and you were both in this bed with me." His eyebrows shoot up and a dirty smirk appears like it's been painted onto his face.

"Enjoy your fantasy. But roll over."

"Not happening, baby girl. You roll over."

Little spoon. Wrong side of the bed. And I still want him to stay.

TWENTY

FIVE-TWENTY-THREE 4-EVER

My room is dark but Hollis is shifting restlessly next to me, clearly awake. "What time is it?" I whisper, unnecessarily. There's no one left to disturb.

"I haven't checked yet. Didn't want to wake you up with the light from my phone."

"So, you decided to just move around until I woke up instead?"

"Felt like the kinder option." He reaches for his phone. "It's five-twenty-three."

"Why are you awake at this hour?"

He spoons me again, aiming to show rather than tell. Oh, that's why. Got it. I object to the hour, but not his condition. "You have lube, baby girl?" His voice has a just-woke-up raspy husk.

"I don't think we need it." I roll over to face him.

"Trust me, we do." He gently turns me onto my stomach (no resistance from me—I've been here before, and he has no trouble finding my clit from any angle), and then I hear the drawer on my side table slide open.

Oh. Now I understand. At five-twenty-three in the morning? This is his idea of anal o'clock? My eyes are barely open.

He holds the tube over me and lets the liquid spill onto my skin. It's cold and I shiver. He laughs. It's low and wicked. Sexy as fuck. The lube trickling between my ass cheeks feels less sexy—until his warm hand follows it, keeps sliding down to rub my pussy. He's going to get me off again before he proceeds to what he wants. I'm still deciding if that's really going to happen or not. We'll see. His fingers press into me, and I tilt my pelvis to increase his access. Two fingers glide easily in and out of my pussy, warm and gentle. His thumb presses up, pulling more lube into its path, and begins to circle the debatable opening. I instinctively pucker, but he keeps tracing the perimeter, and I start to settle, little by little. His fingers inside me feel too good to hold any tension. I'm hazily aware of his third finger being added to my pussy, hyper aware of his thumb entering my ass. Leaving his thumb in place, he withdraws his fingers to concentrate on my clit.

I say his name again when I come, the discordant tone sounding like someone else's voice being forced out between huffs and gasps. And immediately on the heels of that happening, he exchanges his thumb for two fingers in my ass at once. "God, I love the way my name sounds leaving your mouth." The increased stretching and pressure of his fingers eases quickly, until he starts to move them. A fresh application of lube meets his fingers, and he works it in as he keeps talking. "It's been a long time since a woman saying my name has made me feel the way it does when you say it. Is what I'm doing right now okay?"

"Yes." I don't follow with sir because I don't want to say it the way I did last night. I'm not upset with him; it just doesn't feel right like it did then. Hollis doesn't push for it, just keeps pushing his fingers farther inside me with each slow thrust. The pressure is fading again, giving way to a neutral comfort.

"You know you can stop me at any time, right?"

"I know. I trust you."

"I've been lying here awake for a while, hard and wanting

you." He slides in closer to me and heat radiates from his body. His fingers continue to prep my ass for him while he nibbles and kisses my neck, making me squirm. "I love watching your body move against the sheets like that. You still good?"

"I'm good."

I hold my breath for a few seconds when he inserts a third finger, exhale, and relax when I realize there's no pain. He knows what he's doing, and I do trust him, but my breath catches again when he removes his fingers, rolls onto me, positions the tip of his cock, and presses it against the resistant muscle. The groan he emits when he breaches it makes me smile through the discomfort. This man makes me feel sexy in ways no one else ever has. He doesn't just say it; he demonstrates it. And when he so openly appreciates my body or my movements, I want to show him more.

He keeps things at a gentler level this morning, and I find myself rocking back to meet him, despite his size straining my limits. When he picks up a little speed, I can sense the feral appetite he's feeding in the rigidity of his whole body. And when he empties himself entirely inside me, the sounds he makes are ferocious.

I love the self-assured competence he shows the world, and his cocky charm and smart-ass sense of humor he reveals in private, but when he loses all control, comes completely undone like this, I catch myself thinking I could love him as a whole. I don't believe in instalove, and it's not infatuation. It's way too early to be trying to define it, but I don't think I could wish it away if I tried.

"You're a dangerous woman, Oakley Durant."

"Me? Yeah, I'm a real threat."

His breath is ragged behind his laughter. "You have no idea. Let's share a shower before I leave."

"We both know that isn't going to save time."

"Come on, I'll wash your hair."

Well, looks I'm making a stop on the way to the showroom this morning. Nothing says please overlook the time like walking in with hot breakfast tacos. And the smile I'm going to be wearing all day is probably going to broadcast all sorts of things I'd rather keep private.

Before we step into the shower, I say, "Hey, last night when I said sir, I liked it in that moment, but I'm not into it at other times."

His smile is beautiful. *Why is he so beautiful?* "When you said 'sir' last night, I liked it in that moment, too. I like when a woman is submissive in bed, but I'm not into it at other times, either. It's play for me, not a lifestyle."

"Okay. I just felt like I needed to say that."

"I want you to say whatever you need to at any time. Always."

My legs feel heavy from being overworked and over-stretched, but when he begins to massage my scalp and shampoo bubbles cascade down my back, I think I might float away.

While we're drying off, I explain my new protein smoothie regimen to him, along with my goals to start working out again. "Can I make you one?"

"No, I'm good. Did you read the label? Know how much sugar is in the mix? Some of that stuff isn't actually healthy at all."

"Yes. I used to see a nutritionist. I'm well acquainted with reading labels."

"Got it. Consider me butting out of your wellness routine now."

I wrap my towel around my body and leave him to finish getting dressed. With everything tossed into the blender, I set it to high and pop a pod into the coffee maker. I can at least give him some coffee. Hollis comes out of my bedroom in the same clothes he was wearing when he hugged my landlord. It's hard to believe that was just last night. I scrape the last of my smoothie from the blender and drop the spoon into the sink, rinse the carafe, and flip on the garbage disposal. The sink vibrates and the spoon tips right through the rubber flaps and into the disposal before I can grab it.

The riotous clanking of metal sends me scrambling for the off switch. Hollis has his sleeve shoved up and is pushing me aside and reaching in to retrieve the spoon before I can refuse his help. He pulls it out and holds it up. "I hope this wasn't your only spoon."

It's pretty banged up. I'll put it on the bottom of the spoon stack. Hollis reaches for the switch to be sure the disposal still works. Nothing happens when he flips it. "Great. I just moved in and I already broke something."

"It probably just needs to be reset." Laughing, he drops to his knees and opens the cabinet door. I freeze. "Ah, there it is. For future reference, the button is on the back left side. Try it now."

Maybe he won't see it. I flip the switch and the disposal whirs to life. "Thank you. You just saved me from having to admit to Marlise that I'm a menace to all things mechanical."

He doesn't laugh, doesn't make any sound at all. I can't make myself look down to see what he's doing, but I feel him rise up next to me, and tower over me like he does. "Did this come with the apartment or do you always keep your albums under the sink?"

"I didn't want you to see it."

"Why not?"

"Because I didn't want you to think I was copying you."

"I'm not the only person who owns this record. Millions of people own it."

"I know."

"If I introduced you to something and you liked it, why would I feel anything other than happy that we now have that in common?" He sets the album on the counter and steps closer, pulls my arms up and pins them to the cabinet above my head, and moves his face in front of mine, forcing me to look at him. "I hope I can introduce you to lots of things you'll like."

I feel my skin flush from my chest to my forehead. "Maybe I'll introduce you to a few things," I say, aiming for sexy with my tone but it comes out sounding petulant instead. I wish I knew how to cure the malfunction between my words in my head and the way they leave my mouth sometimes, or refuse to.

He smiles. "As surprising as you are, I have no doubt you will." His kiss is sweet. "But moisture is bad for albums, so you might want to find somewhere else to keep that."

"Will do." He accepts my offering of to-go coffee, and I'm not at all worried about him leaving with my favorite tumbler. I know where he lives.

TWENTY-ONE

SOME DAYS YOU'RE THE DISPOSAL & SOME DAYS YOU'RE THE SPOON

Garth glances up from the work table where he's lining up candlesticks when I walk in, takes one look at me, and says, "Somebody got laid last night. Or this morning. Please tell me you got the green hot sauce."

"Of course, I got the green hot sauce." I toss him a foil-wrapped taco.

"No further response?"

"Nope."

"You're no fun at all." He unwraps his taco and holds his hand out for hot sauce.

I drop a packet onto his palm and nod at the candlesticks. "Are you packing these up to take offsite or is someone coming in to look at them?"

"The wedding planner. Your efforts are no longer needed to name her, by the way. We're calling her Cruella DeLil. Her name's Lily. And you'll understand the moment you meet her."

"Am I meeting her alone?"

He takes the first bite of his migas taco and shrugs. "Couldn't be helped. I have an appointment at the only time she could come by. All you have to do is direct her to them. She insists she can't tell me what type of candlestick she likes to use, but she'll know if we have anything that will work when she sees our selection. As if we can't meet with clients and figure out what type of damn candlesticks to use. But it's her *braaaaand* we'll be representing." He rolls his hand and his eyes dramatically. "Put a sticky note on whichever one she picks."

"Or I could open a file and make notes about her preferences. I don't have anyone else coming in today. I'll walk her around and get a feel for her tastes in lighting and finishes. I'm sure she has an opinion on more than candlesticks, and probably a slight aversion to sticky notes. She sounds like a complex woman."

"That's one word for it."

"Did you hate Christian while I was dating him?"

"I didn't like him, that's for sure."

"Why not?" I unwrap a taco for myself.

"He stole your shine. You were this bright, energetic star, and then he came into your life and little by little, you started to fade. When you talked about him, I didn't like what I heard."

"But you never said anything."

"You wouldn't have listened if I had." He brings over one more candlestick and starts staggering them, rearranging and grouping by style and color.

"You're probably right."

"All I know is no dick is good enough to put up with the way he treated you. But I bet his pales in comparison to the one you're getting now."

"Christian who?"

Garth cackles. "Yes! Look at that sparkle in those eyes. Welcome back, girl."

"I definitely feel like I'm headed in the right direction."

"In the direction of being crushed by the most famous thighs in town. You lucky little wench."

"He'd never crush me. Unless I asked him to." I wad up the foil from my taco and throw it at his back.

"Oh, let me get out of here before I slip and fall in your drool."

"Go. Get out of my office already."

I pull a few things I want to be sure to show Cruella DeLil before I sit down to look at emails. I'm feeling bold so I push back on a quote from a vendor and he agrees to my number with no hesitation. We must be in that hot minute when Mercury is out of retrograde because this day is going well. My phone buzzes and I grab it immediately, hoping to see a message from Hollis.

Christian: *Hey, babe. I'm just checking in to make sure you're okay. You haven't posted anything in days and I know your mental health is fragile. How are you? Be honest.*

Oh, he thinks he wants honesty?

Me: *Too busy enjoying my life to worry about posting updates for people who are no longer a part of it. But I don't mean to gloat. I know your masculinity is fragile. Take care of yourself.*

Problem handled. Day back on track. I screenshot the convo and send it to Nadine. She deserves to have a good day, too. She sends back the skull and crossbones emoji, followed by a cactus and a peach, our eternal karmic wish for those who wrong us. And if anybody deserves an ass full of prickly pear spines right about now, it's Christian.

I tell her we need to meet for happy hour one night this week. She agrees but neither one of us picks a date or time. It'll be spontaneous and last minute.

Cruella DeLil is twenty minutes early but I'm not doing anything I can't stop, so I don't keep her waiting. She isn't as difficult as Garth made her out to be, but I can see her inner diva, crouched and ready to pounce if I give her half a reason. I recognize her perfume as Torn from Henry Rose, but I don't point out that I'm also wearing it because I'm not sure she'd like us having something so personal in common. Her need for at least slight superiority is clear. She seems pleased when I compliment the scent, regardless. We share all our reasons for being fans of Michelle Pfeiffer's perfume line. Common ground is always a happy place.

By the time we wrap up, I have a firm grasp on her tastes in everything from candlesticks to buttercreams (French always, never American, unless it needs to be tinted, and then Swiss meringue is best. Obviously.). The woman is not short on opinions, nor is she hesitant to share them, but she's tolerable. And she smells nice.

Jonna swings by to ask if I'd like to do some more field work this week. I try not to jump too sophomorically at the chance to get out of the showroom again, but she knows me. "I promise we're trying to schedule ways we can give you more opportunities, but we're also taking our time hiring anyone else fulltime. We want to make a better decision with the next one."

"I appreciate it. On all counts."

As if he can sense we're discussing her, Christian sends me a text.

Christian: *I wanted to tell you in person but since you can't interact with me without being a defensive bitch, I guess I'll just tell you this way. Honey and I are exclusive now.*

I read it to Jonna because the abject ridiculousness of it is too astounding not to share.

"As opposed to when he was fucking her behind your back?"

"Yeah, from where I'm standing, being in an exclusive relationship doesn't seem to be his strong suit."

"Give me your phone. I will verbally castrate this man-child."

"Thanks, but I've got it. My days of tolerating his narcissistic crap are over."

"It's about time."

"I know. And thanks for not telling me what a dumbass I was when I was still with him."

"You wouldn't have listened."

"You're not the first person to say that to me today. About the exact same issue."

"At least it's over."

"I have no idea why I stayed with him so long."

"All that matters is that you're out now."

"You're right, and as much as I'd love to rip into him, giving him as little attention as possible is what really bothers him." I text back the thumbs-up emoji and leave it at that.

Christian: *It's not like I didn't try to work things out with you. You refused to see me so I had to move on, Oakley. I couldn't just wait around for you forever.*

Me: *Wait around for me? You were seeing her WHILE WE WERE STILL TOGETHER YOU COLOSSAL FUCKWIT!!!!!!!!!*

So much for ignoring him. I know this is what he wants, for me to argue and get upset all over again, and I should be able to avoid this for longer than ten seconds, but yet.

Christian: *You are so emotionally stunted.*

Me: *Oh, please, project some more.*

Christian: *I tried to help you grow as a person while we were together but it's impossible to help someone who doesn't want to be helped. I did what I could. At least I can say I tried. It would be in your best interest to get some therapy, babe.*

Me: *No, I think I'll just keep enjoying the good dick I'm getting now. Don't feel bad that yours didn't do it for me. I'm sure you did what you could. At least you can say you tried.*

Christian: *Please don't cheapen yourself like this. I know you're saying things to try to upset me but if you really are thinking about whoring yourself out to get over me, you need to remember that no man is ever going to want to marry you if he finds out you lived like that.*

Me: *Did you join a cult while I wasn't looking? Seriously, what the hell happened to you?*

Christian: *Your negativity is draining, Oakley. I hope you get the help you need.*

Me: *I hope you fall down an escalator and it rips your dick off.*

Christian: *Enjoy being alone forever.*

Me: *Enjoy being dickless!*

I look up to find Jonna staring at me. She smiles. "It's okay, Oakley. Sometimes you have to get some shit out of your system before you can ignore them."

"Thanks. I'll do better next time."

"Do your worst to that asshole for as long as you need."

"Don't be an enabler, Jonna."

"Hey, I am what I am."

My phone buzzes again and we both jump, ready for a fresh fight. It's Hollis this time. He's headed to Toronto for four days on business and wants to know if there's any chance that I can go with him. The only catch is he just found out he has to go. He's leaving tomorrow.

He thinks that's the only catch? First of all, we are slammed at work. Graduations are coming up and then it's prime wedding month. I can't take off right now. Second of all, I'm not at his beck and call. I need notice even when work isn't this busy. Third of all, we hardly know each other. Four days in a foreign city? That's so much togetherness. But not during the day because he'd be in meetings. So, I'd be what? His evening entertainment? Fucking men! "Why couldn't I have been born a lesbian?"

"What'd he say now?"

"It's not him. It's Hollis."

Her eyes go wide. "Honey, if Hollis Nyx makes you wish you were a lesbian, you might already be one."

"I don't want to be a lesbian because I don't want to have sex with him. I just don't want him to be a man."

"Oh, well, that clears it up."

I laugh. "You know what I mean. I just don't want him to come with all the general bullshittery of men."

"Women come with our own share of bullshit. Don't take your anger at Christian out on Hollis. Let him piss you off on his own."

"He just did."

"No, he didn't."

"You don't even know what he said to upset me."

"You were already upset when you got the message. He didn't have a fair chance."

"I hate when other people are right."

"I know you do."

After she leaves, I call Hollis to tell him I can't go to Toronto with him. He's disappointed but says he knew it was a long shot. "I go to Toronto often. Maybe I can show you around on my next trip."

He just assumes I've never been there. I haven't, but that's not the point. "Yeah, maybe. But I also have a job."

"Didn't mean to imply you didn't. I just thought maybe you got vacation days."

Oh, and you just assumed I wouldn't have plans for all my vacation days already? Just figured I could drop everything to go running off to Canada with you? "I do but I can't use them during our busy times, and this is one of them."

"That makes sense. So, I guess Christmas in Paris is out, too?"

"Unless we're not leaving until Christmas Eve and coming back before New Year's Eve, yeah, that's also a no."

"I don't like your job. Get a new one."

"Excuse me?"

"It was a joke, Oakley. Did I catch you at a bad time? Wait, you called me. Now I'm really confused."

"Sorry. It's been a weird day."

"The spoon in the garbage disposal was an omen, huh?"

"I feel kind of like that spoon right now." My budding anger slips away like water down a drain—no spoon to block it. How does he do this to me? It's like he sneaks up and throws some kind of calming confetti all over me. And why is he impossible to be mad at? That in itself is maddening.

TWENTY-TWO

AN EVENTFUL TWENTY-FOUR HOURS

I never sleep well the first night in a strange place, whether it's a hotel room or a new apartment. This is technically my second night here, but my first to be here all alone. I want to feel empowered and blissed out in my independent woman-hood, but to be honest, it feels a little lonely. And strange.

Maybe it's because my place is still so empty. It doesn't feel real yet. Shopping online for living room furniture and book-marking all the things I want feels hopeful. I can see all the items on my wish list as if they were already here in my space. Envisioning the room fully decorated gives me something to look forward to, a goal. I can't buy it all at once but I can start putting it together little by little. And I can start keeping an eye out for used pieces that have the same aesthetic, now that I know what I want.

When I'm done with my imaginary interior design project, I change into my softest, most worn out sweat pants and an oversized t-shirt, and climb into my bed to watch TV. Now it's starting to feel like home.

Nadine is on another date. Same guy. I've got to get better about remembering his name. It's usually fine if I don't remember the name of the guy she's going out with because she gets tired of them so fast. But I have a feeling this one might be around for a while. Justin? Jared? I scroll back through our recent texts to find it. Ah ha! Jayce.

I think about Christian mentioning I haven't posted anything, and suddenly, I want to boast about my new place. The pic I snap of my bed includes all my new pillows and the soft fringed throw. It looks good, like a bed that would be in a totally put together apartment. I post it with the caption: Back in a place of my own and feeling good! #prettypillows #wholebedtomyself #coralandfloral #noregrets

It takes Christian all of ten minutes to see it and react.

Christian: *You got your own place already? Do you have a room-mate? You've gotten used to having a partner with a higher income to help support you but you have to be smart with your money now.*

Oh, what I wouldn't give for the option to send a throat punch via text!

Me: *I lived alone before I met you. You and I split the household bills evenly. And I made the budget! You're the one who spends every dime you make that doesn't go into your 401k.*

Christian: *At least I have a 401k.*

Me: *Worry about yourself and your new girlfriend. I'm good.*

Christian: *I knew you were upset about that. That's why I didn't get mad when you said those hurtful things to me.*

Didn't get mad? Right.

Christian: *But I hope you realize you're sleeping all alone in that pretty bed because of your own actions. Maybe one day you and I can try again - after you've matured.*

Me: *You and I will N-E-V-E-R try anything again.*

He tags me in a post. Why would he dare? Oh. My. Goddess. It's a picture of his unmade bed with the caption: No one nagging me about making the bed anymore. Life is good! #singlelife #freeatlast

Single? Brain cell, maybe.

～

The new painted and chrome-dipped chandeliers are all hung in the showroom on Friday afternoon and it's nice to have them up and ready to show off, but it definitely highlights how stretched we are for space. We need more square footage, but Jonna and Pepper are fiscally responsible, aka tightwads, so I know we'll be tripping over each other before they finally pull the trigger on a bigger showroom. I think we'll get there soon, though. It's nice to watch this company grow and know I've been a part of it since the early days.

The chime on the door sounds but I'm not expecting anyone else today. It's probably Garth coming by to go over details for the two parties we've got going on this weekend, one college graduation and a fiftieth anniversary. I'm going to both, like I will so many more over the next few weeks. I don't mind the parties as much as the stuffy corporate events. "Hello! Is anybody even fucking here?"

"Honey? What are you doing here?" I step over a disassembled champagne fountain that needs to be put back together and back on display.

"Picking up my final paycheck."

"Nobody left anything with me. I guess Jonna or Pepper knows to meet you here?"

"They said I could come by today to get it."

"Did you schedule a time or remind them?"

"No. It's my money. I shouldn't have to beg for it."

I send a text to Jonna and Pepper. "Jonna's on her way. She has your check."

"Fantastic! Make me sit around and wait on it so I'll get stuck in rush hour traffic."

"It's not a conspiracy. She's on her way."

"Well, she better hurry. I need to get home and pack."

"Big weekend, huh?"

"I'm going to the beach with this new guy I'm seeing."

"Wow. He always told me he hated the beach."

"No, not Christian. Fuck that guy. He claimed I had too

much to drink in front of his friends the other night and embarrassed him. I don't need that shit in my life, so I went home and ordered some tacos for delivery and the guy who brought them to my door was hot. I invited him in, and the next morning he invited me to the beach."

"Hey, a girl can't sit around forever." This explains the uptick in recent texts from Christian.

I message Garth to meet Nadine and me for happy hour instead of coming back to the showroom. He takes no convincing, and as soon as Jonna walks in, I'm headed for my car. She can deal with Honey's surly attitude. There's a dirty martini and a charcuterie board calling my name.

My butt has barely touched the booth cushion when Nadine blurts, "He's thirty-eight."

"Do you honestly think I haven't looked that up by now?" I reach for a piece of cheese and wrap it in prosciutto.

Garth points to the jam. "You want that, I promise. It's spicy."

I take his word for it and add some before I take a bite. "Mmm, that's good."

"For the record, I looked up his age, too," he says. "As soon as I found out you were going out with him."

"What was the acceptable limit?" I ask.

"Told myself I'd stay out of it unless he was over forty-five, but I kind of thought he was late thirties."

"And you love to be right so. . ."

"Almost as much as you do."

The server stops by for my drink order. As she walks away and I look around at all the happy people snacking, drinking, and laughing, I feel lucky. I love this moment right here in this place with these friends. And this jam. "I think it's fig and some other fruit together with jalapeno."

"Apple," Garth guesses. "And I think it might be habanero. Seems too spicy for jalapeno."

Nadine runs her finger through it, licks it off, and says, "It's pear, not apple. But I think you might be right about the habanero."

"Where's Jayce at tonight?" *Yes! I remembered his name.*

"Working late. He's coming by later."

"Here? To hang out with us?"

"No. My place. Way later."

Garth gives a suspicious sounding, "Hmmm. What's his full name?"

"Look out," I say. "Garth will uncover all his secrets."

"Like you haven't already scoped out his socials." She's right. I absolutely have, and he seems okay. So far. Nadine insists Jayce has no secrets and promises I can get to know him Sunday at brunch. Garth promptly invites himself. He's welcome. We used to invite him all the time but he'd always ghost. He probably won't show this time either; it depends on how his Saturday night goes after the anniversary party we're working. "Is Hollis still in Toronto?" she asks.

"Yeah." I chomp on some almonds. "He gets back late Sunday. I still can't believe he thought I could just rearrange my whole life on a whim."

They both nod, but they exchange a glance I don't like.

"For what it's worth," Garth says. "You'd love Toronto."

"You know I couldn't have taken off right now if I'd wanted to."

"I know, but in his defense, he's probably used to dating women who would quit their jobs to accept his offer."

"That's gross."

Nadine shrugs. "It is, but I bet at least a half a dozen women in here have screenshots of his *GQ* cover."

"Or his shirtless *Men's Fitness* cover," Garth says, as if that's the more logical choice.

I've seen the covers. It's not like his age is the only thing I researched. "Well, he was apparently famous, so that level of celebrity worship comes with the territory."

"And you're all good with other women worshipping images of his body, huh?" Garth steals the olive pick from my drink. This is why I order extras. "No jealousy? No insecurity? Just totally confident. Impressive."

Not taking that bait, but nice try, buddy. "I can't control who screencaps an image. Anyway, it's not like we're a couple. We're not dating."

"Right," Nadine says, stirring her drink with her finger but her eyes flit up for a moment.

"Why do y'all keep looking at each other like that?"

"Like what?" Garth reaches for my extra olives but I bat his hand away.

"Like you have a secret. That's the second time tonight y'all've done it."

Nadine sighs. "Oakley, you're dating the guy. It's fine. You can date. There is no official time limit on how long you have to wait after a breakup. Especially when your ex is a dirtbag."

"I'm not waiting for some mandated time limit. But Hollis and I aren't officially doing anything. We've seen each other a few times."

"More than a few," Garth corrects.

"I'm sure he made another call right after I turned him down for Toronto. I doubt he went alone."

"He's been in contact with you while he's been there." Nadine's stare is like a police spotlight; once it's locked on you, you're caught.

"So? It's not like we've been having phone sex. He still could've taken someone."

"He hasn't posted any pics with anyone." And there's Garth, chiming in right on cue to play the role of second investigator.

"Are you stalking him now? He has a right to be with whomever he wants."

"What if he wants you?" Nadine hasn't blinked since they began this interrogation.

"I'm just letting whatever happens happen, okay?"

Garth makes another play for my olives. I deny him again. "That doesn't sound like the Oakley Durant I know."

His words yank a confession out of me. "Sometimes lately, I don't sound like myself to me either. I've been thinking about seeing a therapist, just to sort out some stuff."

Nadine nods. "I think that's a great idea. I'll send you her number."

"Not *your* therapist. I'll find my own. I was already thinking about it, but then Christian mentioned it so I wasn't going to do it, but I know that's stupid."

"Personally," Garth says. "I don't know how anyone survives without therapy. I'm proud of you." He leans in for a side hug and I drop my head to his shoulder for a moment.

Okay, I've said it out loud. To people who will hold me accountable. I guess I'm really going to find a therapist now. "Let's do something fun tonight."

"Like get matching tattoos?" Nadine perks up at her own suggestion.

"I have a strict policy against matching tattoos," Garth says. "With anyone. But I'm not opposed to getting some new ink."

"That's not at all what I had in mind." Now that it's on the table, however, it sounds like the perfect idea. "But I know exactly what I'm going to get." I could draw it myself if I had to; I've designed it once already, but there are plenty of images online.

Nadine sends a message to her artist, and he says he's got two other artists working late tonight and we can all come by in an hour. Only Nade could hit up her tattoo artist on a Friday night and get him to squeeze in three spontaneous appointments. She has given him a million referrals, though, so I guess it's only fair. And I guess we're having one more drink and heading to his shop.

~

The tattoo shop is in an old bungalow-style house, and even with all the sterilization they use and the surrounding restaurants filling the street with the scents of curry and smoked meats and deep fryers, it still has a hint of that musty old-house smell, and the floors creak a little. It's not bad. Gives it an air of authenticity, makes me believe I can trust real artists work here—more counter-culture than med-spa. Not that I have anything against med-spas, but when I want a new tattoo, I want to feel like I'm in the right place. Those super modern, oh-so-sleek shops make me feel like I might have to listen to a pitch for some multi-level-marketing health product before I can get inked. Wrong vibe for me.

When I show the artist an image of what I want, she nods and smiles. "I've done a lot of hats," she says. "But never hers. That's cool. Where do you want it?"

She gets the brim upturned just right to curve over my hipbone, and the six-pointed star is perfectly placed. "Do you want to add your name to it?"

"No. Just the image."

"You're all done then."

Standing in front of the mirror, I admire the perfect edges of the star, and the thin rays emanating from it. Her line work is great overall. This is my only piece with no color, just black lines and some shading, and I like it this way. It's perfect.

"What the hell is that, like a pirate-sheriff's hat?" Garth asks. "Is it a Jean Lafitte thing?"

Tell a guy one time you read pirate smut.

Nadine bursts out laughing. And then she pulls up a pic on her phone of me wearing a hat just like this one. My take on Annie Oakley happened in college, and it was a lot sexier than the photographs I found of her online, including a leather corset, super short denim cutoffs, black thigh-high boots, fishnet stockings, and water guns in my holster, but I figured as long as I got the hat right, my interpretation was valid.

"Oh," Garth says. "Damn, Annie, get your guns. You should definitely wear that costume when you unveil this tattoo for Hollis."

"I didn't get it for Hollis." *Not entirely.* "I got it for me." *Mostly.*

Garth got another snake—he is covered in snakes, but it's somehow not as disturbing as it sounds. This one is rising from a coiled position behind his right ear. "That had to hurt like hell." After my seahorse, I vowed no one would ever put a tattoo gun anywhere above my shoulders again. "Looks good though. Very vibrant. Can't wait to see it after it heals."

"Let's see it, Nade." She smiles at me with her eyebrows raised, and I am suddenly afraid to see what she got. When she starts pulling her shirt collar down, and down, and down, and then over, and over a bit more, my fear skyrockets. "What did you do?"

I exhale when it comes into view. So much better than it could have been. She makes a buzzing sound as she reveals the bees. Bees are her thing lately—bee dishes, earrings, prints on her walls, cutes bees everywhere. Fortunately, there are only three (that we can see) looping across her left breast, heading downward toward her nipple, complete with the little dotted lines to show their flight pattern. "I almost got one more, but I can always add to it. Didn't want to go overboard and make it a swarm."

Garth motions for her to fix her shirt before she flashes the two young guys coming in the door. "You could not possibly have believed we would all get matching tattoos," he says. "Did you honestly think we'd all get bees?"

"Right?" I laugh.

"What are you laughing at?" he asks. "There's not a snowball's chance I would've matched yours either."

"Settle down, serpent king. I need ice cream to take my mind off the burn of my new hat."

I crawl into bed with a burning sensation above my hipbone. It won't be healed by the time he gets home, but it won't burn anymore. Maybe I won't tell him about it, let it be a surprise. Or maybe I'll tell him but not show him right away, tease out the anticipation. Yeah, I definitely need therapy. Everyone who sees my new tattoo for the rest of my life is going to ask me to explain it, and I'm going to think of Hollis Nyx every time I do. *Genius move.*

Looks like I may as well read for a while because I'm not falling asleep anytime soon after that realization. *Maybe I can download a steamy cowgirl story. What if somebody's written a cowgirl and a pirate together? If I find that, I may never leave my bed again. Hollis would make a hot pirate. I wonder if he has plans for Halloween .*

. .

TWENTY-THREE
CLOCK PEOPLE

"I've been to more festive funerals," I say, sidling up next to Garth. "Is anyone here happy that this couple has been married fifty years? Is anyone here even happy to know them?"

"I'm not sure anyone here is happy to be alive. Strangest party we've ever done."

"At least everything looks nice. And the food is fabulous." He cuts his eyes at me. "What? There's enough food here to feed three times this many people, and most of them aren't even eating. They're making me nervous. I stress eat."

"Maybe there's been some bad news in the family and everyone is doing their best, despite the tragedy."

"This event is a tragedy," I say. "How's your new snake?"

"Sore. That's why I have my headpiece on the wrong ear, which I hate."

"Yeah, my hip is still tender, and no less than five people have bumped into me."

"The DJ is almost here. There will be music soon. Surely, that'll help."

"I'm going to duck out for some fresh air,"

"Just admit you're going to steal more food and hide out back to eat it."

"Well, I am now. I wish they'd cut that damn cake already."

I slip into the very short cold food line and fill a plate with fruit, cheese, crackers, and smoked salmon. The hot food pans look like they haven't even been touched. What is wrong with these people? There's prime rib, lobster risotto, a veggie pasta dish, grilled asparagus, roasted potatoes. . .this is an outrageous food bill for no one to be eating.

Two of the catering staff are milling around out back, so I share my snacks with them while we speculate about what is happening here. We spin wild theories, which is a hell of a lot more fun than being inside, but my guilt gets the better of me and I go in to help Garth keep everyone on task. Not that there are many tasks that need doing when everyone just sits at their table. Nothing on the food tables needs to be replenished yet. The champagne fountain is still flowing from the original bottles we poured into it.

I look around at all these gorgeous flowers and it's absolutely killing me that no one is enjoying them. How can you be among this many flowers and not feel even a smidge of joy? Everything is elegant and lovely, the way a celebration of this milestone should be, but the people are all colder than the ice sculptures—grandfather clocks because the couple being feted (however solemnly) owns an antique clock shop.

Hollis sends a text to say he hopes I'm having fun at the party, which is weird because I'm not a guest, but I'm not sure he understands exactly what my job entails. Sometimes, the parties actually are fun; other times, there are hiccups and it's a challenge to keep everything moving smoothly and keep all the problems behind the scenes, hidden from the client, whose peace and happiness we aim to curate and protect at all costs.

Tonight, it's excruciating, even though everything is running like clockwork. Ha! We need an emcee. They could make that joke and maybe lighten the mood in here. Maybe this is just how clock people act? They can't all be clock people, though.

Now I'm picturing them all as walking grandfather clocks, like they normally stand silently in hallways and corners until it's time to chime, but tonight, they've been given a special pass to be people-clocks and come to the fancy party. No wonder they're acting weird. This is their first anniversary celebration outside the home. What if they all start chiming at midnight? Oh, shit. Why'd I have to think that? *Don't start laughing. Don't do it. You cannot stand in the corner laughing hysterically. Think of something not funny. Unfunny. Fuck, I can't look at any of them now without seeing springs popping out of their heads with every resounding bong, and pendulums going haywire and spinning around them like whirligigs. It's too late. The laughter is bubbling up. . .I'm not going to be able to hold it in. . .losing it. . . I have to go back outside. Now.*

I bust through the back door like all the oxygen in the building has been depleted, and I gulp fresh air. And I laugh. This is ludicrous. All of it. But I cannot stop laughing, and it's better that I laugh out here alone like a lunatic than in the middle of the most morose party in the history of all parties.

Garth is standing beside me within minutes. "Did you raid the champagne fountain, too?"

"No, I swear. I just thought of something funny and I couldn't unthink it, so I had to escape to get it out of my system."

"Please share. I could use a good laugh." I tell him about my people-clocks vision, but he doesn't see the humor in it. The more I try to explain, the less funny he finds it, and the harder I laugh. I'm crying when my phone buzzes.

It's Christian calling. *That'll teach me to ask the universe for something unfunny.* I put it on speaker so Garth can hear it. I can barely say hello, but Christian doesn't notice, just launches into what sounds like a very rehearsed speech.

"Oakley, I need you to listen to me. Don't interrupt. Don't

argue. Just listen. This has gone on long enough. I love you. And I know you love me. We've both made some mistakes. We're human. It happens. But I can forgive you, and I think you can forgive me, too. In fact, I know you can. We need to sit down and talk this out. You can tell me anything, whatever happened to make you stop being attentive to my needs, no matter what it was. And I'll be fully honest with you. We both know people don't cheat when they're happy, but I know you didn't mean to make me unhappy. And I'm willing to give you a chance to make me happy again—"

Garth and I make eye contact, and I realize this is the first time anyone else has heard Christian at peak manipulation. And I think I'm hearing it for the first time, too—really hearing it in all its maniacal glory. He got more controlling and preposterous gradually, but now I can hear how unhinged he sounds. He's still talking, but I have no idea what he's saying because Garth and I are both bent over, laughing ourselves speechless. This may be the only thing that could've been weirder than what's taking place beyond the door Garth is leaning against.

"He really said he'll give you a chance to make him happy again," Garth says between wheezing fits of laughter. "And he'll be fully honest with you about what you did wrong." He wipes his eyes. "Holy shit. This is gold."

"And he'll forgive me, too. No matter what I did to make him fuck someone else," I say, and we both cackle. Hours of tension pour from our bodies in waves of laughter and tears. My phone slips from my hand and hits the pavement. I'm laughing too hard to pick it up. "If Jonna or Pepper showed up right now, we might both get fired, but this is the best therapy I could've asked for."

Garth's laughter fades and his expression clouds.

"I'm still going to call someone. I just meant I needed this."

"Yeah, I needed it, too." He opens his arms and I step

straight into them for a hug. "But therapy is a really good thing."

"I know. I promise I'm going to follow through." He holds me for a few more seconds, and I feel steadier when he lets me go than I have all day.

When I finally pick up my phone, Christian has hung up. Hopefully he did it before the therapy conversation. I'm not ashamed of planning to go, but it's none of his business, and I for sure don't want him to think I'm going at his suggestion. I look around. No one else came outside, so there's no fear anyone will report us to Jonna and Pepper for being high on the job. I'm positive that's what it would've looked like when we were laughing so hard. But we are both stone-cold sober, and so much better prepared to finish this event after that release. Plus, the DJ is pulling in, so we now have reinforcements to get this party started.

A little Tony Bennett loosens up the clock people in no time. It's still no rager, but at least I don't feel like we need to check pulses anymore. They're mingling. More of them are eating. A few have braved the dance floor. And the seventy-five-year-old lovebirds are smiling at each other. For the first time all night, they're finally smiling. Their children, who hired us but haven't spoken to us since we arrived, are thanking us and complimenting the food and the venue as if they've been thrilled all along.

Garth and I stay until the last tablecloth is stripped and the DJ is rolling out of the parking lot with multiple servings of every item from the top-tier menu, as well as a few bottles of champagne that never got opened. If anyone deserves them, it's him.

"I'm not going to have any problem falling asleep tonight," I say, as we walk to our cars.

"You better get all the sleep you can. Your tight end comes home tomorrow, and I'm sure he'll want you to be well-rested."

"I don't even know when I'll see him again."

"Oh, we're still doing that? Okay."

"It's true. And he played defensive end."

"Girl, seriously?" He shakes his head. "Drive safe. And thanks for ruining grandfather clocks for me."

"If it makes you feel any better, I'll never look at one the same way again either."

"Never change, Oakley. You're my favorite weirdo."

"You're not the first person to say that to me."

"Never dreamed I would be." He blows me a kiss and gets into his car, but he rolls the window down before he puts it in gear, and shouts, "See you at brunch tomorrow!"

"I'll believe it when I see it!"

I pull out of the lot right behind him, relieved and exhausted. But happy. Really, really happy.

TWENTY-FOUR

EVERYTHING'S CASUAL UNTIL IT'S NOT

Nadine is paying my brunch bill if Garth actually shows. I may have texted him two reminders already. Jayce made it, though he's probably going to start regretting that decision if I don't stop sneaking suspicious looks at him. He hasn't done anything wrong, but I haven't seen Nadine love-struck like this in years. I'm just trying to be sure he's worthy. So far, he's not sending up any red flags.

"What time does Daddy Thick Thighs get home?"

Jayce stops shaking hot sauce over his omelet and holds the bottle in mid-air. "Who?"

"She's dating Hollis Nyx." Nadine steals one of his home fries.

"Whoa. Damn. Really?" Now Jayce has turned the suspicious looks on me.

"Yes, really." *Does he have to sound so shocked?* "I mean, no, we're not actually dating. He gets in around six."

"You're not dating him but you know what time his plane lands?" Jayce manages to put the hot sauce bottle back on the table without taking his eyes off me. "Okay. Are you his stalker or his driver?"

"Neither."

He smiles at Nadine and nods. "She's dating Hollis Nyx," he says.

"I know. That's what I said."

Garth makes an entry and I've never been happier to see him. "Please tell me someone ordered me a bloody mary."

"Only to prove I had faith you'd actually show." Nadine makes the necessary introductions between the guys, and the waitress appears with the large, spicy mary I ordered Garth. I got him the one with all the trimmings, which includes a skewered trio of fried oyster sliders with bacon and avocado. Overachieving menu alert.

We give Garth all the kudos for finally showing up to brunch and he accepts them with a toast: "To unpredictable friends who make you laugh!" He winks at me and I wink back, which makes him laugh so hard he nearly chokes on the first sip of his drink. "Who taught you to wink?"

"Clearly, no one," Jayce says, falling right in like he's always been part of the group.

I tell Nadine about Christian's generous offer of forgiveness last night, and Garth fills in the gaps and adds his own commentary. Jayce shakes his head. "You went from that guy to Hollis Nyx? Way to level up." We all clink glasses again, but there's no way for him to actually know if Hollis is a better person or not. Well, aside from all the documented accounts of his philanthropy and his kindness toward fans when he played for the Texans. I know from my time with Christian that he's generous to his employees. And kind to his. . .whatever I am.

~

My empty living room still bothers me when I come home but my furnished bedroom is an excellent nap haven. I crash with my belly and my heart full.

When I wake up and shake off the post-nap haze, I know

it's time to do the thing I've been avoiding. After an hour or so of reading reviews for therapists, I choose one and schedule an appointment online. Our initial meeting will be a tele-visit, which I like. No need to drive to her office if we're not a match. I go ahead and fill out the new patient paperwork, including the questionnaire about my background, etc. The mere steps of getting ready to see a therapist are emotionally draining. That first appointment is probably going to knock me on my ass. I text Nadine my accountability update.

Laughing at Christian's ridiculousness last night was unavoidable, but I've already had guilty moments of feeling like maybe I was mean, maybe I owe him an apology for treating him badly. Logically, I know he was manipulative and he's the one who treated me terribly, but it's hard to trust my own thoughts when it comes to personal stuff, especially after being told they were wrong for so long—longer than anybody knows. Keeping secrets feels like the best way to maintain dignity sometimes. But self-respect is a different beast. I know my issues go back to before Christian, but he didn't help. Wasn't really his job to help me, but it wasn't his right to hurt me either. It's time to help myself before I backslide.

A hot shower washes away some of the depressive funk I feel creeping in. It's my version of meditation. Maybe standing under running water and telling myself my guilty feelings are uncalled for until I almost believe it is an actual form of meditation. All I know is it works for me. As good as anything I've tried so far, anyway.

Hollis calls when he lands, and I answer too fast to claim I'm anything less than ecstatic. "Please tell me you haven't had dinner yet."

"I ate so much at brunch I probably shouldn't put another bite of food in my mouth for two days." I laugh.

"I'm taking that as a yes, you'd love to have dinner with me."

"Yes, I would love to have dinner with you."

"I'll come straight to your place from here. Be ready because I'm starving."

"So demanding."

"You can't expect a starving man to be overly accommodating."

"Is that a promise that you will be the kinder, gentler version of yourself after dinner?"

"If that's the version you want. I'm half an hour from your door, sweetness."

His voice. That tone. *No sir, I do not want you kinder and gentler.* "I could order food. And we could stay in."

"Pack a bag. I'm ordering food to be delivered to my place. We'll stay in there."

Right. Where there's an actual table to eat on. Makes more sense. "I'll meet you there."

"No, it's no problem to have the car stop at your place. Plus, this way, I get to ravage you in the back seat on the way to mine."

"Right, so our Uber driver can post it and go viral."

"I don't use Uber. We'll have privacy. And the driver will be discreet, regardless."

What does that mean? Does he take a limo home from the airport?

I peek out as covertly as possible when I hear the car pulling up. It's not a stretch limo, but it is a very distinguished looking black car with darkly tinted windows. With my overnight bag in hand, I step outside. Hollis gets out and comes to take my duffle, and he steals a quick kiss during the handoff. My bag isn't heavy, but I'm too happy to see him to refuse his help. And I'm definitely not refusing his kiss.

He stows my duffle in the trunk with his suitcase while I slide onto the backseat. Oh, wow. This leather seat is plush. And there is a privacy divider between us and the driver. So, it's what, a baby limo? I wouldn't even know how to rent a car like this. As soon as he climbs in next to me and closes the door, this backseat feels insulated from the rest of the world. Everything is dark and sensual, and the smell of his cologne is intoxicating, like an aromatic muscle relaxer—specifically, the muscles that keep my legs closed, because they are way too relaxed already.

He pulls me onto his lap, and straddling him is no problem. "I like this dress," he says, as he pulls the material up to bunch around my hips. It's just a simple t-shirt dress, the epitome of casual, nothing special, but it's loose and not constrained by a zipper or any buttons to slow him down. He pulls on the sides of my thong and shakes his head before sliding his hands under me and squeezing my ass. "It's a short drive, and you are wearing way too many clothes." He has my dress over my head and tossed onto the seat beside us before he's even done saying it. That's when he notices it. "What is this?" His fingers trace the brim of the hat and around the star.

"It's a very famous hat."

"Is this Annie Oakley's hat?"

"How'd you guess?"

"Shot in the dark. Why'd you decide to get it?"

"Well, I didn't want to keep disappointing you over and over again."

I slide my bra straps off my shoulders and free my arms, leaving it clasped, but I flip down the cups. His fingers claim my nipples immediately, gently squeezing and rubbing his thumbs across them, opening his hands to caress more of my breasts. "There is nothing disappointing about you." I reach for his belt buckle, and he smiles. "You're going to ride my cock right here?"

"Unless you object."

"We both know better than that, but in the interest of time, I'll take it out for you while you take off those panties you shouldn't have bothered with in the first place." He frees his erection, and I shimmy out of my thong and fling it aside.

Repositioning myself over his lap, my pussy quivers in anticipation of taking him.

His hands grasp my waist to stop me when my delicate skin makes contact with his swollen tip. "Stay right here." One of his hands leaves my side to draw his cock forward and back, mixing his precum with my slickness as he strokes it through my seam. I instinctively rock with the direction of his hand, ready to force myself down onto him, but he changes course, starts to circle my clit with the engorged head instead.

The view of his big, strong hand directing his stiff dick around my swelling bundle of nerves is a scene I could watch forever, but I want him inside me. I shift forward so he's lined up with my opening, and he stills to allow me to show him what I want. Inching down, I savor the stretching sensation he causes.

"Damn, that hot pussy is sucking me in like a vacuum." His head falls back and he closes his eyes for a few seconds while I work every inch of him into place. He opens his eyes and looks at the apex where we meet, drinking in the vision of me sitting all the way down onto his cock, both my legs and my pussy fully opened for him.

His gaze travels up to meet my eyes, and he cups my face with both his hands, sliding them back until his fingers disappear into my hair. "You are so beautiful." The rough edge of his voice makes his sweet words sound carnal, and that, coupled with the darkness his widened pupils have created in his eyes, reveals a man the public doesn't know at all.

This is not Hollis Nyx, famous football player, gregarious philanthropist, and cutting-edge businessman. This is the animal that comes out to feed after the paparazzi and fans have all gotten their quotes and their photos. That side of him is sincere, but this side is hungry. And I am ensnared beyond all hope of escape. One look into the molten depths of his eyes and I can tell he's deciphering me, too. It doesn't matter what I tell anyone else, or even myself, because he already knows.

When I rise up and begin to pump my hips, there is no way to prevent my clit being palpated, and no matter how much I want to focus on him, it continues to swell and draw my attention to the tingling that's building there. His jaw is tight and he's thrusting up into me now, not letting me pull away. He's close, though. I know he is. I bounce faster and he thrusts harder.

And then the car slows. "We just turned onto my street."

"Already?"

"Unfortunately. Fix your clothes, but don't get too comfortable in them because they're coming off the moment we get inside."

I hurry to get my bra back up and my dress pulled down by the time we roll to a stop at the curb in front of his house. I'm still in the backseat after Hollis is finished removing our bags from the trunk. He peers in at me with raised eyebrows. "You coming in?"

"I can't find my underwear."

"You don't need them."

"Do you think they could've slipped into the crack between the seat?"

"I don't care where they went. All I care about is where we're going." He extends his hand to help me out of the car, and I slide across the seat toward him, consigning my lost thong to the abyss.

The driver didn't lower the glass when we arrived, but he waits for us to walk into the house and close the door behind us before he pulls away. "I really thought you were going to be able to finish before we got here," I say.

"No way. But I thought you might."

"Wait. You were holding back?"

"Hell, yeah, I was."

"What were you thinking about to keep it from happening?"

"I just left an airport. That's a theater of unappealing sights and behavior. What were you thinking about to fend off your orgasm?"

"You."

He clutches his chest dramatically and staggers back a few steps. "I've been shot."

"I meant I was thinking about how badly I wanted you to come." My words tumble out with my laughter. He steps closer with a sly grin on his face, proud of himself for amusing me. I reach for the buttons on his shirt. "You were the class clown, weren't you?"

"No," he says in a serious tone. "I couldn't be anything other than perfect, on the field and off."

Enough of his buttons are open now that I can slip my hand inside to rub his chest. "I have to admit, I do appreciate your perfectionism."

"Oh, yeah? Do you?" The playfulness wends its way back into his voice. "Maybe you can show me that perfect appreciation in a special way." He wraps me up in his arms and walks me back toward his kitchen.

"What exactly are you asking for, player?"

"No, I'm the coach now."

"So, you think I need coaching, huh?" I back-step out of my shoes.

"I think you need to play."

"Do you have a position in mind for me?"

"A few." He lifts my dress over my head again.

"I think I'd make an excellent kicker."

"Not even an option." He unhooks my bra with one hand.

"Impressive finger agility, coach. I could maybe be the safety?"

"If you can tell me what the safety does, I'll work my agile fingers in your tight little snatch until you're saying my name and gasping for air."

"That's easy. The safety is the one who rides out on the little cart with Gatorade to keep everyone safe from dehydration. Right?"

"I think we've found the real class clown."

My back meets the hard edge of the stone countertop on his island. "Well, I am hilarious."

He devours my mouth with his kiss. "You're delicious is what you are." With one hoist, he has my bare ass on his countertop. He lifts my legs to plant my feet there as well, and then he opens my knees like he's cracking open a new book, gently, appreciatively.

"What position is this?"

"The easiest one. All you have to do is lie back and relax. Like you're waiting for the little cart with the Gatorade."

Within minutes his agile fingers and warm tongue have me panting like I could use some damn Gatorade. And before I've even caught my breath, he's lifted me off the counter, set my feet on the ground, and turned me around. My cheek and chest are pressed against the cool stone. He pulls my hair hard enough to lift my head so he can see my face. "Didn't I do a good job? Show me. Offer your pussy to me."

I arch my lower back and he groans. "Yeah, that's my good girl."

His fingers release my hair and I utter a mewl of protest. "You didn't want me to let go? You want me to pull it while I fuck you?"

"Yes." He fists my hair and tightens his grip. "Yes, sir."

The way he's grinding into me and smashing my hipbones into his counter, Annie Oakley's hat may be colored with blues and purples for a week. But the tension of my hair in his fist and his deep groans and labored breathing have me suspended in a place where all I can feel is pleasure.

Everything he held back in the car breaks loose. I love

feeling the telltale swell inside me that signals his imminent orgasm, those few seconds when I think I might not be able to take him anymore, that it's too big, too much, and then sweet mercy arrives for both of us. I may not always come when he's inside me, but I always feel an adrenalin rush when he does.

My legs are almost too shaky to stand on but I have to pull away from the counter to give my new tattoo a reprieve. Hollis holds my back against his chest. His breath is still irregular but his arms are firm around my waist. "I missed you," he whispers against my cheek.

"I'm glad you're home."

"You want to sit in the hot tub? My back could use a good soak."

"Can't. New ink."

"Oh, shit. I shouldn't have had you pressed against the counter like that. Why didn't you say something?"

"I was fine."

"Hey," he says, turning me to face him. "I like to be rough, but I never want to actually hurt you."

"I'm not hurt."

"I know what a new tattoo feels like." He sighs. "Can I get you some ice?"

"Actually, if you could just get me a towel right now, that would be great."

He laughs. "How about I carry you to the shower?" Before I can answer, he's carrying me down the hall.

The doorbell rings while we're still drying off. I'd forgotten all about food the moment he lathered up my hair. Hollis pulls on a pair of sweatpants and goes to the door.

We accidentally eat standing at the kitchen island where he crushed my hat less than twenty minutes ago. The original plan was to take our food to the dining room table but we started unpacking it and talking while taking bites to taste everything, and the next thing we knew, we were done.

Our next plan was to watch a movie in his bed but I've

been talking his ear off since we crawled under the covers. He muted the sound and he's been listening attentively but I really didn't mean to catch him up on every detail of my life from the past four days. I skipped any mention of Christian's reconciliation offer, and everything else that involved him, but I've been talking about myself for way too long. Time to shift the spotlight. "What did you mean earlier when you said you had to be perfect on the field and off?"

"It's what my dad expected. He was a hard man, bitter about a lot of things he didn't get to do. He had unyielding expectations of his family. My mom was supposed to be the perfect wife and mother. My sister could barely breathe he was so goddamn oppressive with her. And as soon as I put on the pads in peewee league, I became his son, the football player. It was part of my identity from that moment on, and there was no excuse for me to be anything less than the best. By the time I started high school, it already felt like a job."

"Did you ever like playing?"

"I loved it. I was the happiest little kid in the world when I put on those pads for the first time. But I didn't understand that I wasn't ever going to be allowed to take them off again. I love football to this day. Still go to as many games as I can. But I could feel myself becoming resentful about all the things I didn't get to do because I'd had to eat, sleep, and breathe it for so many years. I was done. Didn't want to become him, miserable and angry. So, I found a new goal to chase. A new way to live."

"Did your dad understand?"

"The Texans drafted me right out of college. Twenty-two-years-old and I was a first-round pick on a twelve-million-dollar contract. Five years later, my signing bonus was nearly that much on a contract with a twenty-three-million-dollar guarantee. When I decided to walk away, I was a healthy free agent with offers on the table. My father never asked me why or what my plans were. He just looked me in the eye and called me a coward and a failure, went on to spare no words in telling me what a disappointment of a son I'd always been. And he died of a heart attack six months later. I got to live the dream of playing in the NFL, still hold two league records, own a successful global company, and have a current net worth of ninety-million-dollars. And my father died disappointed in me."

"Hollis, I am so sorry."

"Don't be. I didn't tell you all that to make you feel sorry for me. I told you to explain that my father was a man who couldn't be pleased. Nothing would've ever been enough for him. I think he was broken long before I entered the world. And this was probably way more than you really wanted to know."

"I promise it wasn't." I wish I could take away all his hurt. He speaks about his father so matter-of-factly, but his eyes dim. That's pain, the thief that steals your shine. "For what it's worth, you're a perfect kisser, in the car and out."

His laugh is lighthearted, and I don't know how after everything he's just revealed, but he smiles at me and says, "Are we watching this movie now, or what?"

"Finally. I've been trying to watch this movie since we came in here."

I lay my head on his chest, and he turns up the volume on the TV, holds me tighter, man-spreads and drapes a thick thigh over mine. "Flag on the play," I say.

"For what?"

"Taking up too much space on the field."

"That's not a real call."

"It is, too. It's a personal foul."

"What's the penalty?"

"No morning sex."

"I should've known you'd end up being a ref." He takes his leg back.

"The head ref."

He smirks. "Morning head. Even better."

"I didn't offer that."

"It's in the job title. I don't make the rules."

Somewhere, there's probably a couple lying in bed together actually watching the movie they started without spontaneously starting new conversations every two minutes. Couldn't be us.

TWENTY-FIVE

THE PRICE OF HAPPINESS

I'm rushing to get my shoes on and grab my purse because Hollis forgot to mention he had an early meeting this morning (he says he told me, but he's wrong), and of course, he won't let me take an Uber. "I'm going to worry all morning that you were late to your meeting because you insisted on driving me to work."

"They'll wait. I just don't want to keep them waiting too long." He holds the door open for me, but he shuts it right before I get there. "And they're going to have to sit a little longer because I forgot something."

"I can't wait for you in the car?"

"No. You have to wait right here."

I huff because I've apparently hurried around for nothing, and now he's running back to his bedroom. He reappears holding a small violet bag with a silver fleur-de-lis embossed on it. "I got you something while I was in Toronto."

"Why?"

"I saw this in the store window and it made me think of you. Hope you like it." There is a small box inside that matches the bag, and when I open it, I find a silver necklace with a seahorse pendant. The tail has several different colored jewels set at random intervals. The moment I see it, the seahorse on the back of my neck tingles with the memory of his first touch, when he traced it and sent an electric current down my spine. When I ask him to help me with the clasp, and he touches it again, my breath catches and my eyes water.

Fuck, this is the sweetest thing. It's perfect. I blink and take a deep breath. "Thank you. It's beautiful, Hollis. I don't know why you did it, but I love it."

"I did it because I wanted to." His big thumb swipes at a rogue tear cresting my cheek, and for some reason, that makes me want to cry buckets. "It looks good on you."

"We should get going." I sniffle.

"Not yet." He kisses me and I'm not sure my feet are touching the ground anymore. His smile when he breaks the kiss keeps them floating. "Now we can go."

"Wait. I need to ask you something that's really none of my business but I'm not sure, and if I don't ask you directly—"

"Oakley, you can ask me anything."

"Are you seeing anyone else?"

"No. I'm glad you asked. I sometimes take for granted that everyone operates like me. I've been conditioned my whole life to have a singular focus, and I know not everybody moves through the world that way. I can get fixated on what I want, come across a little intense sometimes." He runs his hand through his hair. "My turn, I guess, huh? Are you seeing anyone else?"

"No."

"I haven't forgotten that you just got out of a relationship, but I can't help what I feel. I like you. I want to spend more time with you. But I don't want to make you feel smothered or trapped so if I—"

"Maybe we could just let whatever happens happen?"

"Yeah, let's try that." He kisses my forehead. "And let's get to work."

∽

The showroom is buzzing when I walk in. Jonna, Pepper, and Garth are all drinking coffee and laughing. "Did I miss a meeting?"

"No, I'm just filling them in on Saturday night's anniversary party." Garth glances at the paper cup in my hand. "Oh, I see how it is. You got the good coffee and left us to fend for ourselves." He lifts his J & P Events mug.

"You've mastered that coffee maker, Garth. You're a pro now." I drop my purse on the table we all share as a makeshift desk. "Hollis drove me in this morning. I couldn't ask him to buy coffee for everyone and I knew he wouldn't have let me pay and I didn't want to make it a whole uncomfortable thing."

"Do you have any idea much that man is worth?" Jonna asks.

"It has recently come to my attention that he has a net worth of ninety-million dollars, an amount that boggles my brain, but I would still prefer to buy my own coworkers' coffee."

"You're nothing if not hard-headed." Pepper laughs and shakes her head. "And that's why we love you."

Garth stands up straighter. "Hello, pretty, pretty little jewels. Someone has a new necklace. Come here."

I step closer so he can see my new bejeweled seahorse, and he immediately flips the pendant over. "That's what I thought. Damn, girl. At least you let him buy you nice jewelry."

"What do you mean?"

"That's from Delphine's."

"It's expensive?"

Jonna cackles. "Not if your net worth is ninety-million."

Garth sighs. "You are completely clueless, aren't you?"

"I know it's pretty and it was really sweet. Oh, damn. I

don't want him to think I like it because of where he bought it."

"Don't worry. I'm sure he knows you're oblivious." Garth refills his coffee.

"Or to put it a nicer way," Pepper says. "You're not shallow enough to be swayed by designer labels. He bought it for you because he can easily afford it, not because he thought you'd care about the store."

"Who you calling shallow?" Garth cuts his eyes at her and they share a laugh. I want to join in, but I'm in a state of shock, which is exacerbated when Garth turns to me and says, "Seriously, you probably need to increase your renter's insurance to make sure that's covered."

"Jesus, Garth! How much do you think this thing cost? Should I even be wearing it around?"

Jonna gives me a side hug while giving him the side-eye. "He's fucking with you, Oakley. It's wasn't cheap, but you should absolutely wear it."

Pepper stands and stretches. "Okay, let's get out of here and get some work done, leave Oakley to Google the price of her necklace in private." They all laugh as they gather their things.

"I'm not going to do that." They're still laughing as they go. The box is in my purse so I take a pic and send it to Nadine.

Me: *Does this box mean anything to you?*

Nadine: *It means I can't afford whatever's inside of it. What did he buy you? Show me now!*

I send her a pic of the pendant against my chest.

Nadine: *Your seahorse! I'll cry. Tell me again how you're not dating.*

Me: *Shut up.*

Nadine: *Just looked it up. Do you want me to tell you what that necklace cost?*

Me: *No.*

I don't need her to tell me because I'm looking at the answer on my own computer screen, thank you very much. And it's more than my rent. My phone dings with a calendar reminder.

Me: *Just got reminded I'm having lunch with my mom today.*

Nadine: *I didn't know she was coming to town.*

Me: *She's only here for the day. Meeting with an attorney to negotiate something in her latest divorce settlement.*

Nadine: *She had to come all the way to Houston for that? No good attorneys in Dallas?*

Me: *Not good enough apparently. Wish me luck.*

Nadine: *I'll light a candle. Burn some sage. Do a dance. Sacrifice some donuts.*

Me: *Enjoy your donuts. At least I have that therapist appointment to look forward to later.*

The Fed-Ex guy walks in and looks around like he's searching for a place to put something. "Where do you want them?" he asks.

"That depends. What are you bringing in?"

"A couple thrones."

"Thrones?"

"That's what they look like to me."

I walk outside with him and, yep, that's what they look like to me, too, even through all the layers of plastic wrapped around them. When I told Jonna people were asking for thrones for their wedding receptions now—thanks to a certain celebrity who keeps trying to outdo her last wedding with every new set of vows she takes—I thought she'd get oversized wingbacks we could also use for clients not requiring an actual throne replica, but she went all out. There's no multi-purposing these babies. And they'll probably stay reserved six months in advance. "Just set them inside. I'll unwrap them and make a space for them later."

Thank goodness I'm meeting Mom at the restaurant. These things are the exact level of tacky that would have her itching to say "I do" again. She hasn't actually cosplayed a queen at one of her ceremonies yet.

I'm not busy so I try to help him bring the thrones in and discover immediately they are ridiculously heavy. He's taken them off the truck already but when I attempt to push one forward on the sidewalk, I can't make it budge. "Are they made of actual bronze?"

"I've got it. I'll bring them in with the hand truck."

Did he flex his biceps when he said that?

With the second chair inside, I thank him and offer him a bottle of water. He accepts my offer, unscrews the lid, takes a big gulp, and then he asks me out. I don't know this guy. We've barely spoken. He usually drops boxes and goes, hardly even makes eye contact. I'm positive I've never flirted with him or given him any indication I was interested in him. He leans against the doorframe like he has nowhere to be, no schedule to keep. "I heard you on the phone the other day talking about your recent breakup. That's how I know you're single."

"Oh, I didn't realize you heard any of that conversation. This is awkward, but I'm not actually single anymore."

"Got back together, huh?"

"No, it's someone new."

His smile is sheepish. "You can say you don't want to go out with me without having to make up a fake boyfriend." He doesn't say it defensively. I think he honestly believes I lied about seeing someone to validate turning him down.

"He's not fake."

"Quick, what's his full name?" He says it teasingly, but I don't mind telling him.

"Hollis Nyx."

The drink of water he just took burbles back out his lips. "Right." He laughs. "And I'm dating all the Kardashian sisters."

"No, I'm serious. He bought me this necklace." I lift the seahorse as if proves something.

"That's very cute. It looks just like something Hollis Nyx would buy." He screws the cap back on his water. "Thanks for this. Enjoy the rest of your day."

"Hollis Nyx did buy it!" I yell at the truck as he drives away. What makes him think he would know what Hollis would or wouldn't buy?

Mom's already halfway through her first glass of chardonnay when I sit down. "You look tired," she says. "And puffy."

"Puffy? I do not look puffy. What does that even mean?"

"Oh, goodness. I didn't mean to ruffle your feathers. Have some wine." She pushes a full glass toward me. I hate chardonnay but she's taken the liberty to order for both of us so I take a sip.

"How did your appointment with the attorney go?"

"It went well. I like her. She's a real pitbull."

"I'm sure she'd be charmed by the comparison. My landlord's an attorney, but not that kind. I think she mostly represents athletes."

"That's nice." She has her face in the menu. When she sets it down, she looks at my face again and says, "How's Christian doing?"

"We broke up. I told you. That's why I have a new landlord."

She swishes her hand through the air like she's clearing cobwebs. "Yes, I know, Oakley. That's why I'm asking how he's doing. Heartbreak affects men differently, especially when they're young. They don't bounce back as easily as we do."

"Heartbreak? He cheated on me, Mom."

"He's young and attractive. Well-educated, good job, nice car. . .it's no surprise someone would've tempted him."

"He and I are the same age. I also have a degree and a good job and a car. But I didn't feel the need to cheat on him." She opens her mouth and I put my hand up between us. "So help me, if you say it's different for men, I will walk out of here."

"Honey, he programs computers for a huge company. You help people pick out tablecloths for birthday parties."

"Yeah, well, I'm sleeping with the man who owns that huge company." Honestly, she'll probably be prouder of me for this than anything I've ever done.

"Hollis Nyx?"

"Yep, that's the guy."

"Well," she says with a smile. "Good for you. That must've been some night."

"It wasn't a one-night stand. We're actually seeing each other."

"Sweetie, be serious. That man has dated super models."

"And now he's dating me."

"Oakley, you're smarter than that. He's too old for you, anyway."

"He's only thirty-eight."

"And you're twenty-three."

"I'm twenty-six."

"Oh, good Lord. Stop making me feel old."

"Why is it so hard for you to believe he would want to date me?"

"I'm sure he finds you very attractive, your youth certainly not being the least of the attraction, but he's accomplished things most men only dream of. Men like that don't settle."

"My whole life I've watched you chase wealthy, successful men. You've said things like, 'It's just as easy to love a rich man as a poor one,' to me since I was a child. Did you think any of those men were *settling* for you? Because I'm pretty sure you saw yourself as a fucking prize they were lucky to have on their arm."

She swirls her wine and stares into the glass.

"He bought me this necklace when he was in Toronto last week. It's from Delphine's. Does that mean anything to you?" I feel sure she'll recognize the store. She knows her luxury brands.

"It means he can afford to buy you expensive trinkets. He probably does that for every pretty young thing that spreads her legs for him. I wanted more for you. I wanted you to have something solid, like you had with Christian. And you're ready to piss it away because you can't forgive some stupid fling. You'll wake up one day and realize pride makes for a cold bed."

I slide my wine glass to the middle of the table. "Well, right now my bed is hot. And I'm damn proud of myself for a number of reasons you couldn't begin to understand. I hope the attorney gets you everything you want, Mom. Drive safe going home." I push back from the table.

"Name one substantial thing you have in common."

"We both know what it's like to be raised by a bitter, broken parent." Yanking my purse strap from the back of my chair, I turn on my heels and walk away from her.

I have the afternoon off for my therapy appointment. I hope this woman is ready, because I finally am.

TWENTY-SIX

SHELTER FROM THE STORM

I close my laptop and pour a glass of wine, relieved at how well my first therapy visit went. She's probably going back and writing notes on top of her notes after the way I shared like I was emptying a firehouse. We only had time to hit the highlights of situations because I jumped around a bit, but she said it was okay to do that in the beginning.

The only time her expression changed was when I told her about Hollis. I didn't tell her his name, just referred to him as someone who used to be a local celebrity. Her disapproving look couldn't be masked, and I know it's because of the recent breakup. Even I can look at it objectively and see that leaving an emotionally abusive situation and walking right into a new relationship isn't normally ideal. But you can't help when you meet someone. I'm trusting Nadine on this one. It's okay for me to date Hollis.

Marlise is leaving in the morning for a business trip and I'm on plant duty, which apparently requires training. I take my wine and walk across the backyard to learn what it takes to keep a few plants alive.

Except she doesn't have a few plants. She has a house full of them. And I'm also going to be responsible for the ones on the back deck and the front porch. This is much more than I expected. But still, it's pouring water. Pretty sure I'm up to the task. "Wow, you could open your own garden center."

"Yeah, I got a little carried away during the pandemic, but I've kept them all alive this long so I can't fail them now." *No pressure. Thanks.* "I keep them mostly grouped by type and watering needs. I've made note cards for each section but I thought it'd be easier if we walked through it together once."

"Sure." I should've brought more wine.

I'm not actually worried until we enter her bedroom and I see the orchids. So many orchids. "I should probably tell you I don't have a great track record with orchids."

"People kill them because they think they need more care than they do. Orchids are easy." She points to a notecard that says: Feed Weakly Weekly (Thursday). "You put them in the tub, use the shower sprayer to water gently but thoroughly. Basically, you want to get the leaves rinsed and the potting mix moderately wet, spray on the orchid feed that's under the sink, just a few spritzes on the roots, let them drain complete, set the pots on towels to finish drying. Use the brown towels, that's what they're for. And that's all there is to it." That sounds way more complicated to me than she seems to think it is, but I nod. I only have to feed them once. How much harm could I do?

As if the orchid room didn't make me anxious enough, she leads me into her office and I see my absolute plant nemesis: succulents. She's probably already afraid I'm going to kill her orchids. I keep my mouth shut about my history with succulents. Again, she makes it sound so simple. Thank goodness she wrote out these note cards. "Got it?" she asks after we cover the most delicate looking group.

"I think so."

"You'll be fine. You only have to water everything once, just different days. Sorry about that but when I staggered the watering schedule, I had my own schedule in mind."

"It's no problem. Renting me that apartment earned you unlimited plant watering." As we walk back toward the door, I see the wall of photos I hadn't seen when we came into her office. They're all autographed.

"Ah," she says. "You've spotted my wall of fame."

"Are they all clients?"

"Every one. Have you found him yet?"

My eyes land on him as soon as she asks. "He looks so young."

"Hell, he was. That's his rookie year. A lot of these pictures are rookies." She shakes her head. "Babies signing multi-million-dollar contracts before their brains are even fully formed. He was smarter than most. Never got in any trouble. Never spent himself into a hole. I used to worry some of them were never going to settle down and grow up. With Hollis, I worried he was never going to learn to relax and enjoy any of it."

"How long did it take him?"

"I'm still waiting." She flips the light off and leads me to the outdoor portion of my training.

I can't shake what she said about Hollis not being able to relax and enjoy his success. That's now how I see him at all. He works hard, but I think he genuinely enjoys it. He's driven, but he can relax. I've seen him do it.

Nadine loves hearing about the watering schedule and the note cards, but she is also sure the orchids and succulents are in grave peril on my watch. She's not crazy about my therapist's reaction to my dating Hollis, but when I explain that I'm not deterred by it, she lets it go. My mother's performance, on the other hand, she cannot let go. She rages in my defense and I love her for it. Her outraged support bolsters my courage. I didn't sense it flagging, but I can feel myself sitting up straighter, my shoulders un-rounding as she reiterates all the things I already know about my mom's insecurities, and the way she projects them onto me. Sometimes, you just need to hear it from someone you trust.

By Wednesday, Hollis has apologized no less than four times for working so much this week and not being able to see me. I like that he's so ambitious. I'm not jealous of the time he spends working, and I for sure don't miss having someone constantly checking up on me and being passive-aggressive about the time I spend with my friends. Friday night can't come soon enough, though. I do want to see him.

I brave the orchids on Thursday, and though I have to revisit the note card three times, I feel like I got it right. Marlise didn't say I had to wash the brown towels but I don't want her to come home to laundry. She works almost as much as Hollis—mostly from home, but I see her office light come on early every morning and it stays on until late at night. I think someone should worry about when she's going to relax and enjoy life.

The FedEx guy won't make eye contact with me when he drops off six boxes of lightbulbs Friday morning. Pepper wanted to be sure we had options on hand to show clients how versatile our lighting options are. We now have everything from blacklights to rainbow painted bulbs to bulbs with filaments that looks like a flame to emulate a gas lamp. Garth comes into the showroom in the afternoon and helps me decide which bulbs to display in which lamps and chandeliers. He digs out extension cords with rolling switches on them so we can easily flip them on and off without having to crawl behind tables and shelves to swap plugs. This is tedious but much less so with a partner. "You seeing Hollis tonight?"

"I am."

"What are your plans?"

"Dinner and drinks. Then home. Probably his place. I think he's more comfortable there than at mine."

"Oh, stop. You're depressing me. Give up and get married already."

"You know I don't care about clubs. I got all that out of my system in college."

"You're too young to be so old."

"We have fun."

"I hope so. There are hundreds of women in this town who'd love a chance to show that man a good time."

"I'm well aware. I had lunch with my mother already this week, remember?"

"Oh, do not paint me with that brush." He stands after plugging in the last cord, dusts off his pants with his hands, and hugs me. "Enjoy your subdued version of fun to the fullest. I will be dancing the night away."

"That's right. No event tonight."

"I am a free man. Look out, Houston. Here I come."

"Don't injure yourself. We do have an event tomorrow night. And I have plans."

"Your concern is overwhelming."

I hug him again. "You know I love you. Go live your wild life. Shock me with all the details on Monday."

The jeans Hollis is wearing tonight look like they were custom made for him. He might actually have his jeans custom made. He's definitely not walking around on off-the-rack thighs. After dinner, he brought us to a rooftop bar downtown. I've been here before with friends but it feels different with him, sexy with the sky so dark and the outlines of surrounding buildings all aglow. Not to mention the abundance of lights strung around us here and the smattering of stars still visible between the rolling clouds. And his thighs in those jeans.

Speaking of thighs, his hand just found mine. "I like all your little black dresses."

"I only have two, and now you've seen them both." I take a sip of my drink as his hand inches up my leg.

"I like them both."

"If you don't stop doing that, you're going to get us both in trouble."

"Nobody's watching. They're all in their own worlds. Why can't we be in our own little world?"

"Because we are very much in public." I squeeze my thighs together to capture his hand before he ventures across the border from teasing into doing.

"Maybe we should get out of here then, go somewhere private."

I down the rest of my drink. "I thought you'd never ask."

There's thunder in the distance when we emerge on the sidewalk below, definitely a storm rolling in. The sky's casting ominous purple threats and the lighting hasn't even started yet. I love a good thunderstorm but I prefer the safety of being indoors when it hits. We may have lingered over our drinks too long to escape this one.

Sprinkles prickle my arm. He takes my hand and we run for his car parked at the corner. The rain picks up and I squeal as the cold droplets coat my bare shoulders.

"My place," I say, shivering in the passenger seat. "It's closer than yours."

"My office is closer than both. It was the first private place we shared, and I'm feeling a replay of that."

"I need to dry off though."

"There are towels in my office, remember?"

Oh, I remember every detail from his private bathroom, but the memory of a washcloth is much more vivid than the towels.

"But I can't lie," he says. "I prefer you wet." His hand finds my thigh again as he merges onto the freeway. "You can hang your dress up to dry in the bathroom but I plan to keep your pussy soaked." He slips his fingers inside my panties to get a jump start on the task.

I loosen my seatbelt enough to rise up onto my knees in

the seat. He buries his fingers inside me, but that's not why I changed positions. When I turn my body and lean forward, making it clear my head is heading for his lap, he pulls his hand forward with his fingers inside me to urge me closer, and the intense pressure he exerts in that spot makes me want to freeze and have him repeat the motion, but I wouldn't tease him like that, not right now.

His erection springs free and I lick around the head before dragging the tip of my tongue through the crease and flicking it back and forth a few times. He groans and I glance up to make sure his eyes are still on the road. When I slide my mouth over him, his hips rise to force a few more inches between my lips. He's finger-fucking me fast and rough but I take my time sheathing his cock. And then I suction my cheeks in tight to trap it there and pull up slowly, lowering just as patiently, maintaining the contraction around him, and repeating the steps as I begin to twist my head, creating a corkscrew motion that has him lifting out of his seat again.

The windshield darkens and I know he's pulling into the parking garage. I feel sure we're alone here so I keep sucking his dick but I release the pressure, let my cheeks go slack to free the saliva that's built under the force. My mouth glides freely as I uncover him all the way to the tip, my spit coating him and creating wet sloppy sounds as I take him again.

I want to be in control, to own him, but his hard strokes inside my pussy are sparking intense vibrations through my core and my clit is starting to hum with that tingly sting, the *stingle* that ushers in epic orgasms, the type that turn my breath to rapid mini screams like the ones leaving my mouth around his cock as my pussy spasms on his fingers. I come making the *O-Face* of dirty memes but I have no choice because my mouth is far from empty. His cock has reached maximum swell. It twitches twice before it lurches in my mouth and spurts his come at the back of my throat. I swallow as fast as I'm able while still trying to catch my breath from my own orgasm, and doing my best not to choke in the process.

His back collapses against the seat, and I let my head lie heavy on his lap while we both recover. There is nothing, but yet everything, sexy about this moment. I think there is sweat mingled with the raindrops on my skin now, and his, too. He reaches down to play with my hair and I could fall asleep right here. The air conditioner blows over my damp neck and I shiver. "Let's get you inside and out of this wet dress."

I push myself up from his lap. "We weren't in the rain long enough to soak my dress. I think it's mostly just my hair that's wet now."

"No, it's not just your hair." He removes his fingers from me and brings them to his mouth. Watching them leave his mouth as he slowly sucks them ensures it's not just my hair.

The elevator feels like it's been refrigerated. Hollis envelopes me in his arms and it's like being wrapped in an electric blanket. "How are you so warm?"

"I've always put out a lot of body heat." He tightens his arms.

"Well, you have a lot of body so. . ."

He laughs. A lot, huh? His office is dark except for the small lamp on his desk. Rain runs down the windows and throws snaking shadows at the wall. His shirt is already off and he's kicking off his shoes. I reach back to pull my zipper, but even when it's at the bottom, my form-fitting dress doesn't fall open. I still have to peel it from my body and shimmy it down my legs. Hollis bites his bottom lip and sucks in a breath. I smile at his visceral approval.

My dress doesn't need to hang dry. It's fine, but my panties are done for the night. I let them fall to the floor and lay the dress across the back of a chair facing his desk. Holli's jeans join my dress. His shirt's already been draped over the adjacent chair.

He holds my naked body to his chest and I listen to his

heartbeat. "That was incredible, by the way," he says. "In the car."

"Yeah, for me, too."

"Come on. I want to kiss you in the rain." He takes my hand and leads me to a glass door I never saw the first time I was in here. It's in the corner on the wall that meets the windows we were looking out then.

"You have a balcony?"

"I do." He slides the door open and motions for me to step outside. It doesn't overlook the back area where employees congregate on breaks. It's on the side and faces a wooded area with no pathways leading into hiking trails, no water fountain, or bridge, just nature. There is an overhang from the roof so the rain isn't hitting the concrete where we stand, but falling in front of us like a thin curtain. I am standing outside completely naked and I don't feel an ounce of hesitation or wariness. Hollis is holding me. The only sounds are the falling rain and our breathing.

Thunder rolls and it's not so distant now. The lightning illuminates the rain but it's not close enough to be dangerous. The air isn't cold, only the raindrops, and we're protected from them here. He kisses me and the warmth and safety of him heats my spine.

We could be anywhere, standing outside like this, kissing while a storm picks up around us, and it wouldn't feel any better than it does right now, here on the side of this office building in Houston—closer to a freeway than an ocean or river, no church bells ringing or gorgeous old architecture as a backdrop. Nowhere special. Except it is. Everything is special with him. He presses me against the wall and deepens the kiss. His hands are everywhere and my leg is hooked around his waist but, aside from our mouths, our bodies are only making surface contact. My nipples are hard under his thumbs and I shoot up onto my toes when he pinches them. He smiles against my mouth, breaking our kiss, and then he peppers quick kisses down my neck and chest until he can pull a nipple into his mouth to suck on it.

I hold his face to my chest and begin to push my hips forward, an open invitation for his cock but he steps back and turns me around. His hand slides up my back, pushing me forward until I bend at the waist and my hands find the railing. He starts to fuck me with long hard thrusts, keeping it slow but not gentle.

My hair tickles across my shoulder blades. Hollis gathers it in his fist and pulls to tilt my head back farther. "Such a dirty girl, being fucked on the balcony, not caring if anyone sees."

We both know no one is likely to see us at this time of night, but the reminder that someone could does make me feel dirtier. If anyone happened to see the way this massive man is slamming his cock into me right now, I'm sure they wouldn't look away. I'm not sure I'd shy away from being watched either.

"Would you like it if someone saw us out here like this?"

I just thought that exact thing so it should be so easy to say yes, but I can't. All I can do is bite my lip and try to focus on how good this feels. And then, with no warning and no conscious effort at all, my shoulders lift in a meek shrug, and I hear myself say, "Maybe."

He kisses my ear and whispers, "I love the fantasy, too, but that's all it is. I'd never push beyond that. Just want to know you, what you like thinking about." His strokes take on an easy rhythm, less forceful but no less deep. Powerful muscles drive his hips forward and back like he could do this all night. Meanwhile, my legs are already feeling weak and my low back is starting to burn, but I'm not ready for him to stop either.

The rain falls harder and the wind shifts, blowing it slant, sending lashes of cold water against our skin, stealing my breath when they land. His hands grip my hips to hold me in place when I flinch. He increases his pace as if he's determined to prove to the wind and the rain that he's going to finish this, regardless of what they throw at us. And he does.

He carries me inside to the bathroom, which I could start to expect if he isn't careful. The warmth of the washcloth chases away my chills. We dry off and he wraps his towel around his waist. I pull mine up under my arms, wrap and tuck. "Nothing is better for warming up than whiskey, and I've got the best. If I'm pouring, are you drinking?"

"I could be persuaded." I sit on his couch, the place where he first put his cock inside me, and pull my feet up, stretch to reach for a pillow, snagging it by the corner and dragging it back across my lap.

"You and pillows," he says, shaking his head as he hands me the glass. He sits on the end of the couch and pulls his legs all the way up, spreads them and tells me to lie back between them. I relax against him and sip his good whiskey, slowing warming from the inside out.

"Saw your autographed rookie photo this week."

"In Marlise's office while you were watering her plants, I presume."

"You were a cutie."

"I was a maniac. Constantly in trouble. She was always having to bail me out of jail, bribe judges, falsify court documents . . ."

"Yeah, that's pretty much what she said." I laugh and twirl his arm hair between my fingers. "Did you ever have a wild streak when you were young?"

"Not one I could act on. Not trying to imply I was a saint by any means, though. I just had no freedom to take stupid chances at the age everyone else starts doing it. I didn't escape it entirely. Went through a pretty selfish phase in my late twenties, got a little self-destructive for a while, too. Maybe it was for the best I couldn't act out when I was younger. At least I was old enough to snap out of it before I did any lasting damage to me or anyone else."

"Do you ever feel like being held back the way you were caused any damage?"

He's quiet behind me for a few beats. "Yeah, I guess in some ways it probably did. I sure don't have anything to add to the conversation when people start to reminisce about all the wild stuff they did in high school or college. What about you? Were a good girl back then?"

"No. I was a wild child. A very lucky one. I didn't think so at the time, but looking back, I definitely had a guardian angel or two. Having no one hold the reins at all does its own kind of damage."

"You had a lot of freedom growing up, huh?"

"I had no one bothering to worry if I was messing up. My mom was too busy with her husbands."

"She had more than one?"

"Not simultaneously, but she was never single for long."

"I wanted more freedom and you wanted less."

"I didn't know that's what I wanted. But yeah. The conversations I can't add to are the ones where people talk about the things they weren't allowed to do, how they couldn't go to that one big music festival with all their favorite bands, or pile into a car headed to the beach for Spring Break with no parents, or have their curfew extended for prom."

"Your teens years sound like a constant party."

"It's all a blur." I laugh. "Not really. If I'd been a different kid, things might not have turned so well for me though. I knew I had to keep it together on some level. Maybe because I wanted more out of life, or maybe just because I knew I was the only one who was watching to make sure I didn't go too far. But I can't say I denied my wild streak. That would be a lie."

When he gets up to pour us more whiskey, he brings the bottle back with him, along with a blanket he pulls out of the trunk serving as a coffee table. I gasp. "You've been holding out on me! You had blankets in there all along?"

"Hey, I can't just share my blankets with every slutty girl I drag up from the company picnic."

"That's probably why you have company picnics, so you can steal your employees' wives and girlfriends."

"I draw the line at wives."

"Open season on girlfriends, though."

"You were already an ex-girlfriend. Unless you lied about that." He uses his leg to tuck the blanket around mine.

"I didn't. We were over. You really didn't do anything bad in high school?"

"Not in high school. But one time in college, me and my roommate dined and ditched at an iHop."

"Did you go back later when you were alone and pay the bill?"

"No. I thought about it, but I was afraid if I went back in, they'd recognize me and call the cops. So, I just never ate at that iHop again. It was right by campus, too, and I always had to come up with excuses why I couldn't eat there because it's where everybody always wanted to go."

I'm howling. I can't even attempt to hold it back. "When did you go from the guy who was making up allergies to pancakes to avoid prison. . . " I have to pause to laugh again. "To the dirty talking, hair pulling, sexually confident guy I met?"

"Oh, that's just who I am. I didn't have to learn any of that."

"In other words, you watched a lot of porn in college."

"Who didn't?"

"Did you have the same girlfriend all through high school?"

"I did. Did you date the same guy?"

"I did not."

"It's funny now, but skipping out on that bill at iHop could've changed my whole future. I was on an athletic scholarship with no money to back it up if I blew it. My dad wouldn't have kicked in a dime for my education if I'd lost my scholarship. It was actually a bigger risk than it sounds like, and a whole lot stupider."

"You did one bad thing, and you couldn't even enjoy the rush of getting away with it. You're still ashamed that you did it, aren't you?"

"Honestly? Yeah. Did you ever do anything you regret?"

"Yeah." I trace the teeth of the skull on his forearm. "I understand regret."

He squeezes me between his thighs. "Don't regret me, okay?"

"I don't know how anyone could."

TWENTY-SEVEN

CHECK YOUR MESSAGES

The last thing I remember, we were laughing and kissing in the dark while thunder shook the windows, but his office is incredibly bright on the other side of my eyelids now. I open them to see the clear morning sky outside. "Fuck! We fell asleep. Hollis, wake up." I roll off the couch and crawl until I can stand. "Shit. Shit. Shit."

He sits up, calmly rubs his eyes, and looks around until he spots his phone.

I tug my dress up over my hips and he steps behind me to get the zipper. "I've gotta go. If someone sees me here, doing the walk of shame out of your office—"

"I distinctly remember you telling me last night you weren't ashamed of me." He laughs, but I can't. This isn't funny.

"Like it or not, you're still famous. People love gossip. And I don't want to be part of anyone's gossip."

"I understand. I'll drive you home." He has his clothes and his shoes back on before I can even make a decision about my underwear. *Do I wear them or trash them? Put them in my purse?.* "Take a few minutes to wake up and calm down. I'll go down and start the car, and you can come down when you're ready.

That way there's no chance anyone will see us in the elevator together, okay? But I promise you, nobody comes in this early, especially on a Saturday. Except to use the gym and that's on the second floor. We're on the third so you won't meet anyone headed up. It's all good."

Christian used to do that, come in early to work out. Thank goodness he started hitting the gym after work instead. Or hitting up Honey, whatever he was doing.

I splash water on my face but my rained-on-slept-on hair won't be helped by anything other than a full shower. He has a coffee maker and paper to-go cups in his office so I drop in a pod and brew myself a quick wake-up dose.

The elevator arrives quickly, and I breathe easier once I'm inside. I'm sure Hollis is right about there being hardly anyone here. And we're not together, so no one will even know who I am or why I'm riding down in the elevator looking like a swamp monster. The elevator car slows to a stop and I look cautiously at the number panel. Second floor. Great, someone must be done at the gym already. *Geez, what time did they get here? Psychopath.* I tell myself it might not even be an employee; it could be the custodial staff.

And then the doors open and I'm confronted with the biggest lie I ever let myself believe. He sneers and pulls his head back. "Oakley? What are you doing here?"

"Don't worry about what I'm doing," I say, with all the poise of a defensive twelve-year-old.

Christian steps onboard. Any normal person would've declined in this situation, waited for it to come back after I was gone, but of course he doesn't. "You look like shit."

"Huh, I feel amazing. Better than I have in a few years, actually." I take a gulp of my steaming hot coffee and it scalds my tongue, but I'd sooner eat glass than do anything other than smile.

"Are you on drugs? Have you been up all night?"

I ignore both questions. The doors open and I step off, but

he stays rooted in place, staring after me. "I talked to your mom the other day. She's worried about you."

You asshole. Don't you dare start colluding with my mother. I turn around to face him before I leave the building. "Is that what we're doing now, Christian? We're playing messenger for other people in our lives? Oh, okay, then. Your boss says, hi!" I salute him with my coffee cup. "How do you like that message?"

I push through the front doors and stomp toward the parking garage without so much as a backward glance. *Talked to my mother! Like hell she's worried about me! I've got a message for her, too!*

Hollis's car door is lighter than I remember, so it's a whole lot easier to slam. "Sorry."

"Bad trip in the elevator?"

"You meant that to be funny, but you have no idea."

"I didn't want any coffee, thanks."

"Here." I offer him the cup.

"It was a joke. Apparently, I should stop with those this morning."

"The elevator opened on the second floor. Apparently, Christian's gone back to using the gym in the morning now that we're not together anymore."

"Oh. And he's probably the last person you want to know about us."

"No, I don't care if he knows. I'll tell him myself. *And by that, I mean I basically just did.* But he's been talking to my mom!"

"Damn. He's hitting up your mom?"

"I look nice, but I will punch you."

"I've seen you look nicer, to be honest."

I bite the inside of my lip to keep from smiling, make a fist and show it to him.

"Would a bagel help?"

"Donuts."

"You got it, sweetness." He reaches over and rubs the back of my neck.

"Or you could take me to iHop."

"Too soon."

"Listen, I've got dirt on you now. I'll call the FBI and turn you in."

"I forgot to spank you last night. That's what's wrong with you."

"Bold talk from the Rooty Tooty Fresh and Fruity bandit."

"Keep it up and see what happens when we get to your place."

"Sorry, but I don't think I can invite you in. My landlord's an attorney. I'm sure there's a clause in my lease about not harboring fugitives on the premises."

"I told you I was a bad boy. You didn't want to listen." He winks. When I return the gesture, he says, "See, that right there should be a crime."

We laugh. He buys me cheap, greasy donuts. They mean every bit as much as the expensive necklace he gave me.

And his sweet goodbye kiss means the world.

TWENTY-EIGHT

WINNING STREAKS DON'T LAST FOREVER

Hollis is headed home to shower and then back to the office for the day. He insists he has no choice after being gone last week. I fall face-first into my bed to finish sleeping, but I can't stop thinking about Christian and my mother talking behind my back. Nadine is the only one who will fully understand.

Me: *Late lunch today?*

Nadine: *I'm not even out of bed yet and you're already thinking about lunch. Two o'clock? Mexican?*

Me: *Perfect.*

Now I can sleep.

~

My mother doesn't factor into the rest of my weekend. Saturday brings tacos and margs with Nadine in the afternoon, and sushi and sex with Hollis in the evening. He stays over at my place, makes the requisite quip about all my pillows, but manages to enjoy his time in my bed just the same.

Marlise knocks on the door Sunday morning around nine,

which is unusual. I hope I didn't kill an orchid or a succulent. Or if I did, that it wasn't some rare specimen, but my fears are all unfounded. She invites us over for breakfast.

Seeing her and Hollis together, it would be easier to believe they were mother and son, rather than attorney and client. She cares about him beyond his legal wellbeing. His mother is still alive, but he hasn't volunteered as much about her as he did his dad, and I don't want to pry.

When he asks if I want to spend the rest of the day together, I tempt fate and mention a museum exhibit I want to see. It features preserved human bodies to showcase the inner workings of muscles and organs and the effects of health and lifestyle choices. I'm fascinated by the concept but Christian and his superficial friends all think it's disgusting and morbid. Hollis says, "I've been wanting to check that out, too." He pulls out his phone and buys tickets on the spot.

"I was afraid you might think it was weird."

"Oh, it is. But I'm into your weird."

We eat again right after we leave the museum. "I don't think I've ever dated a woman I could take straight from skinless bodies to Mediterranean food."

"I strive to be memorable."

"You succeed."

He stays until late Sunday night, watching TV with me in my bed—okay, we don't actually watch much of anything but each other. He finally decides to go home so he doesn't have to drive twice in Monday morning rush-hour traffic, and I completely understand. But after he's gone, I wish I hadn't agreed so easily.

"If I keep walking in to find y'all huddled together like this, I'm going to develop a complex."

Jonna looks up from her coffee. "If you keep showing up late, I'm going to have to replace you."

"Sorry. Traffic was awful. There was a wreck."

"Don't listen to her," Pepper says. "You're irreplaceable. And you get to be a mess when you're falling in love. Comes with the territory, but it also comes with a time limit."

"I like the irreplaceable part."

Garth rolls his eyes. "She's still in denial about the rest of it."

"You did get my email about today, right?" Jonna asks.

"I haven't checked email yet."

"I sent it last Thursday."

"Oh. I guess the end of last week got away from me." I open my phone and read the email as if this is the first I've heard of it, not mentioning that I saw it come in Thursday afternoon, but forgot to go back and read it. "I'm meeting with two caterers and scoping out a renovated hotel ballroom. Got it."

"Good. Your first appointment is in forty-five minutes. You've got just enough time to get there."

"Guarantee her tank's on empty," Garth says, laughing because he knows me too well. And he's right, but I'll make it. It's not my first day driving in this city.

The first caterer has food samples for me to try, and she's made things from her brunch menu. I skipped breakfast this morning so I love her already. The second caterer just wants me to hear his pitch while he shows me photos from events and sample menus on his website. He's accomplished, and very proud of himself. It's close to lunch time when I leave him and I'm not too far from Nyx International.

I've never been the type of person to drop in on someone at work, but I think Hollis might be the kind of guy who wouldn't mind it. Plus, like I said, it's close to lunch time and I wouldn't turn him down if he offered. Lunch, I mean.

His personal assistant, Greer, buzzes him to let him know

I'm here. She has to ask my name, which feels weird but shouldn't. How is she supposed to know who I am? "You can go on in."

He's at his desk but he stands when I push his door open. "Damn. Has anyone told you today that your tits look great in that shirt? No, don't answer that. I don't want to have hunt anyone down."

"You say the sweetest things. I was hoping maybe you hadn't had lunch yet and I could steal you away for a bit."

"I would love that, but we're having a major computer problem that could become an emergency if we don't get a handle on it pretty damn quick. I'm waiting to hear back from IT to see if they can cure the issue or if we need to escalate to our contract IT security team. It wouldn't feel right to leave while I've got them all working through lunch and reporting to me every fifteen minutes with udpates."

"Plus, you have to okay the call to outsource it if they can't take care of it." *Christian talked enough about his job that I remember things, even if I don't fully understand them. The contract IT security firm is insanely expensive, but Global shipping can't get backlogged, I know that much.*

"Right. But you can hang out here with me and I can order something."

"I could do that."

"You have a preference?"

"Surprise me."

"Remember you said that." He sits on the front edge of his desk to place the order, and then he motions for me to come closer. I step between his legs and his hands slip under my shirt. "I need a better view," he says, pushing it up above my bra. "Black lace, my favorite color."

"Lace isn't a color."

"Says you." He shoves my bra up to free my tits completely. I've had them bare in this office before but never when someone was working just outside the door. I feel like a teenager making out on someone's couch when their parents could catch us any minute, not that I think anyone would enter his office without knocking. Or without an appointment, probably.

He kneads and squeezes while we kiss, and I run my fingers through his hair. His kisses on my neck turn to nibbles and I'm sure he knows I'm powerless when he does that. But my spine arches like a cat to pull away when he ducks his head to kiss lower. With a firm hand, he pulls me back in and closes his gifted mouth over one nipple while he thumbs the other. I continue to play with his hair, enjoying the fleecy feel of his beard against my breast, noting the contrast of that softness compared to the roughness of his thumb against my skin on the other side. It isn't calloused, but his hands aren't soft. Nothing about him is soft, except his nature. Under the hard muscles and fierce drive, he's all heart.

And he is oh, so very skilled at casting spells on my body with his harsh touches and crude words. Nothing feels wrong when it's him doing it, not even this fondling session, midday in his office with a potential corporate crisis looming. I close my eyes and get lost in the enjoyment of his attention.

"Disaster avoided! James sent me up to say he'll buy lunch if—" My brain is still processing the sound of the door opening as Christian's triumphant voice continues to invade the office.

I yank my bra down, and then my shirt. Hollis is standing tall next to me but I can't look up at him. I can't move, can't speak, can hardly breathe.

Christian yells loud enough for people in the courtyard outside to hear. "Jesus Christ, Oakley! What are you, an escort now? Is that how you're paying your rent?"

"Hey!" Hollis's voice booms like thunder as he advances on him.

I scurry to get between them, pushing against Hollis's chest. "Hollis, don't. He's leaving." With an imploring look over my shoulder at Christian, I keep talking. "He's going back to his department. Just let him go."

"Clean out your desk when you get there. Your services are no longer needed."

"You can't do that." My head snaps back toward Hollis. "You don't want to fire him over this. It will be an HR nightmare. A PR nightmare! Everybody needs to cool off."

"No, fuck that. I quit." Christian storms out.

Shit, this is bad. "Christian, wait!" I run after him and catch him in the hallway. "You love your job. You can't quit because of this."

He won't make eye contact, just stares at my chest. "You'd barely let me get close to them. *Too sensitive.*" He uses air quotes to emphasize his mocking imitation of me. "I guess if a guy's got enough money, you can play through, huh? I thought you were special, but you're trash." He meets my gaze now and there is pure vitriol in his eyes.

"You don't really think that about me. You're just mad and hurt, but please, don't be stupid enough to quit your job."

"You're right. I'm done being stupid over you. You were never worth it in the first place. I should've listened to my mom. That won't last, by the way—you and him? He's out of your league, babe."

"Fuck you."

"No thanks."

I keep my head down as I pass Greer's desk this time. Stepping back into his office, I close the door behind me.

"You love him," he says.

"No, I absolutely do not. But I can't stand the thought of either one of you doing anything so shortsighted because of me. You can't fire him, Hollis."

"I built this company. I own it. And I decide who works here."

"You're angry and I appreciate that, but firing him would be a mistake."

"Won't be the first one I've ever made, and I'm sure it won't be the last."

"If you think I went after him because I cared how he felt about me being with you, that's not it. I promise."

"Well, you cared about something to go running after him like that."

"He and I are over. Done. Completely."

"Cool. He's still fired."

"I really think that's a bad call."

"You've made that clear."

His voice is so cold. And the way he's looking at me isn't much better than the way Christian glared at me in the hall. I've never seen him like this. "I'll go. Give you some space."

He turns his back to me and walks to the windows.

I have less than an hour before my last appointment of the day. Nothing could matter less to me right now than the gaudy carpet and foldable dividing walls of a hotel ballroom. But I will pretend to be wowed. I will make notes of any pertinent information we might need. I will ask all the necessary questions. I will get through this.

I'm numb by the time I walk into the hotel lobby. The woman's mouth moves as she shows me the renovations, but I can't hear the words coming out. I nod along as if I'm listening raptly to every detail, but all I can hear in my head is Christian screaming. All I can see is Hollis turning his back on me. I hate this ballroom. I will never recommend it to a client.

But I am a professional, staid and decorous. I shake her hand and thank her, feign appreciation for the swag bag full of branded products and treats she gives me before I leave. I hate this entire hotel, from its fine dining restaurant to its onsite chocolatier to its spa—all the way down to its hypoallergenic bamboo sheets. Trash.

Sitting at a redlight, I roll down my window for fresh air. The car next to me has theirs down, too, and "Tiny Dancer" is blaring from their speakers. The driver is singing along and

I join in—softly, slowly. Two strangers sitting at the same light in a city of over six million people, singing the same song, but we couldn't be more disconnected.

I don't even know how long I've been sitting in Nadine's driveway when she gets home, or why I didn't text her, why all I could do was drive here on autopilot and wait for her to pull me out of the drivers' seat and hold me together.

TWENTY-NINE

NO DERAILMENT WITHOUT WRECKAGE

"Go ahead. Tell me I'm an idiot." I hug Monk-Monk tighter and sniffle against the back of his head.

"I not going to lie to you, Oak. You shouldn't have gone after Christian. It's not your job to coddle him. It never was. But Hollis will be reasonable once he's had some time to cool off."

"Why is it that I can do things with him that I couldn't stand with anyone before him, though? Maybe there's some truth in Christian's take. I put Hollis on a pedestal because of his status, see him as superior. And that makes me subordinate to him by default."

"That is entirely different from what Christian insinuated, like not even in the same universe. Sure, part of why things feel different with Hollis probably is psychological, but maybe it's that you trust him more and can relax more with him than you ever could with Christian. And for the record, you didn't see him as superior in the beginning. Hell, you hardly even know anything about his past or his fame. But you knew he was a good guy."

"I thought he was, but the way he became such a bully so fast. . .the way he looked at me. I don't know."

"A bully? He took up for you. And himself, which he had every right to do. Let's not forget Christian is his employee and there is still an inherent power dynamic there, even when the boss is a nice guy. Christian barged into his office and called you a hooker, which also implied something derogatory about Hollis."

"He told me his mom always thought I was trash."

"He was lashing out, trying to hurt you. And who gives a shit what his mom thinks? She raised an asshole."

"My mom loved him from day one."

"And he saw from day one how impressed she was with his expensive clothes and car. Christian knew exactly how to manipulate your mom, just like he knew exactly how to—" She stops abruptly.

"Manipulate me? You can say it."

"I don't need to. Let's order junk food. How about loaded tater tots and fries with green-chili queso?"

"I'm not hungry."

"That wasn't part of my question." She orders, and I stare into the depths of her empty fireplace like I expect to find answers there, while I ignore my buzzing phone. It's probably Christian, calling to yell at me for getting him fired.

I eat a few bites of the greasy, cheesy potato combinations Nadine has unpacked and spread out on her coffee table, but I have no appetite. In fact, if I eat much more, I'm positive I'll be sick. "Thanks for letting me unload all my emotional instability on you," I say, wiping my hands with a Spud Crud napkin. "I'm going to go home and take a hot shower to wash away this day."

"You know you can dump all your baggage here anytime. Are you sure you're okay to drive?"

"I am now."

~

My apartment feels like a void, but I walk straight through the emptiness to the sanctuary of my fluffy bedroom. A steamy shower drains what's left of my energy, and I crawl into bed, leaving every throw pillow on it like a fortress around me.

I get up to pee, and I've definitely missed the sunset. My phone says it's 1:12 a.m. One minute earlier and I could've made a wish. Too many to choose from. I have missed messages, and I'm awake now so, why not?

The two from Christian are vile. I delete them without responding. The smarter thing would've been not to even read them, but too late. They'll live in my head with the rest of his words for a while.

There are three from Hollis:

Hollis: (7:36) *Please let me know you're okay.*

Hollis: (9:52) *I reached out to Marlise to make sure you made it home safe. I'm sure you hate that but at least I know your car is in the driveway. I'd still like to hear from you.*

Hollis: (11:46) *He had no right to talk to you like that. I'm not sorry.*

Who asked him to be? My phone buzzes in my hand, as if he knows I'm reading his messages. I toss it onto the bathroom counter like it's burst into flames. My resistance holds until I'm back in bed. From the safety of my pillows, I read his latest.

Hollis: (1:16) *I meant I wasn't sorry for my reaction to him. I'm sorry we didn't get to eat lunch together. I'm sorry I let you leave like that.*

Me, too. I turn my phone off.

The sun cuts like a laser through my bedroom blinds. The birds are outside the window are happily chirping and I despise them for it. This morning came too soon, but I go through the motions and get myself ready to face the day ahead.

Humidity slaps me in the face as soon as I walk outside—

right before the vision of Hollis leaning on the hood of my car, holding two cups of coffee makes me question if I'm hallucinating. But no, he's as solid as ever, and parked behind me so I have no choice but to talk to him. I glance at Marlise's window, certain she's seen him out here and probably thinks he's adorable. "I figured it was the least I could do." He holds one of the cups up for me. "After texting you all night."

"You didn't keep me awake. I turned off my phone."

"Can't say I blame you."

"Okay."

"Okay."

I step close enough to take the coffee. "Thanks. I really need to get to work on time. I've been late a lot the past few weeks."

"The last thing I'd want to do is put your job in jeopardy." He abandons my hood, but just keeps standing there in my way. "But I do want to keep seeing you."

"Hollis, we both know that's a bad idea."

"Why?"

"Because. . .you're you. . .and I'm me. . .and we're not the same."

"A real reason, Oakley."

"You've dated supermodels!"

"One. I dated one supermodel, and her job had nothing to do with it."

I give him the incredulous look he deserves for even trying to say that.

"I was initially attracted to her looks, yes. Just like I was with you. That's how human sexuality and attraction works. But I dated her because I liked her as a person. Just like I do you. She and I dated long enough to realize things weren't going to work out between us, but you and I haven't done that yet."

"I live in your attorney's garage."

He returns the incredulous look. "You live in a nice apartment in a great neighborhood. You're not squatting in somebody's abandoned shed."

"You're not who I thought you were," I say. "You're vengeful."

"Hmmm, interesting. Why'd you come up to me at the company picnic again?"

"You called me over to you." I do the come-hither curl with my finger to remind him.

"And there was nothing vindictive in your motive for going up to my office with me, huh? That picture on his phone? Didn't fuel anything?"

"You were fully complicit in my vindictive plan. You took me up to your office because you knew I'd be easy to fuck."

"Sure as hell did. Yep. Not even going to try to deny that." He takes a drink of his coffee and the tattoos visible under his rolled sleeve draw my eyes, the same way they did at the picnic when he drank his beer, raised his cup to me. "But then I got you up there, and you didn't react to me with any awe, never once mentioned football or some interview you'd seen or any online bullshit. . .you were just so goddamn real and honest, but there was nothing simple about you. You were complicated, and I wanted to decode every mystery you held, learn all your secrets, and do whatever it took to make you keep smiling at me, laughing at my dumb jokes."

"I'm not exactly the manic pixie dream girl you're making out to be."

"You know, I've never been entirely clear what that term means, but I can assure you I don't see you as any sort of manic pixie anything. Although I have to admit, I think the dream girl part sounds promising." He gives me his sexy, sly smile but it only makes me feel sadder.

"And I think you have white knight syndrome, and you met me at a vulnerable time. But I don't need saving, and when I'm back to myself and you realize that, my strength will end up being a huge turnoff, and you'll move on to the next damsel in distress. It'll be easier if we face the truth now." I click the fob to unlock my car doors.

He steps aside. "You couldn't be more wrong. Nothing turns me off more than a woman who can't make her own way in the world. But I think it's okay for two people to need each other sometimes."

"I don't need you, Hollis. It's been fun."

"You can't push me away that easily. But I'll give you some time."

Garth pulls up to the showroom right after me. I never even saw him in my rearview. Not sure I checked my mirrors at all on the drive in, to be honest. I'm fine.

He eyes the logo on my coffee cup. "She doesn't even need to use her boyfriend as an excuse for not taking her coworkers' coffee orders anymore. She's simply too famous to bother now."

"He showed up in my driveway with it this morning." I'm not ready to get into everything's that happened. It won't hurt to let my work family think I'm still seeing him until I'm ready to talk about it. "And in what world am I famous?"

"Have you really not seen it?"

I struggle to get the key in the lock. "Seen what?"

He steps inside behind me and flashes his phone screen at my face.

Oh, damn. Someone took a photo of Hollis and me at the rooftop bar, and it's online now with a cutesy caption about Hollis Nyx and his new "arm candy." I'm nobody's vapid arm candy. Gag. But we do look happy, laughing against a stormy night sky. It's a good shot. They even caught the lightning in the background. *What a metaphor for what was to come.*

"People are so rude." I fling my purse at the table. "The man is entitled to some privacy."

"Not in public, he's not. Anyway, you look hot. I'd make it my profile pic if I were you."

"I'm happy with the pic I'm currently using."

"Suit yourself. How'd your appointments go yesterday?"

"The first caterer was my favorite but they're both good options. The hotel was awful."

"Really? I have a friend who works there and he has done nothing but rave about all the changes and their new amenities."

I remember the swag bag is still in my backseat. "Hold on. I've got something for you." When I come back in with the bag and offer it to him, he lights up. "The chocolate is probably ruined. I forgot to take it in when I got home."

"I can live without the chocolate," he says. "But please tell me that candle is in here." He rummages around. It's an ample bag, lots of stuff, but I didn't go through it. "Yes!" He holds up a small jarred candle with the teal filigree of their logo on the label and removes the lid. "Mmmmm, smell this." I take a whiff. It's not bad. "It's their signature scent. I could roll around in this candle."

"Keep your kinks to yourself."

He continues to explore the contents of the bag, drops a tube of something called Lick My Lips on the table in front of me. "Please replace your cheap lip balm with that. Thank me later."

Garth heads out to oversee the setting up of a college graduation party taking place on the lawn of a historic mansion this afternoon. Location, location, location. It'll be a sweat fest, but at least the gorgeous building in the background of their photos will look impressive. I have a few hours before my first appointment shows up. A surprise sweet sixteen consultation. The doting moms are always hard for me. All their gushing excitement over their kid's next birthday and lamentations over how *grown up* their *baby* is now feels performative to me. Kids grow up. It happens. But sixteen ain't it.

I try the lip product Garth left me while I stare at the computer screen. With the picture enlarged, I can see a stray strand of hair that had blown across my right eye, making me squint. I'm so close to him I may as well have climbed onto his lap. We're tipsy and bordering on tawdry. His hand is on my thigh, and his thighs look even bigger than they really are from this angle. And they're not the only thing that looks big in the shot. *Do not read the comments. You already know they're all speculating about what's in his pocket. World's oldest, lamest joke.*

The CPA is asking for last month's receipts so I busy myself scanning them.

After the sweet sixteen consult—the worst: a crier—I run out to get myself some lunch. I come back to a note from a florist stuck on the door about a missed delivery. It indicates they'll try again.

The Fed-Ex guy brings boxes I'm not expecting, says he saw my picture online, and apologizes for not realizing I'd been serious about dating Hollis Nyx. *Can I not go two hours without someone mentioning him, I swear!*

I'm locking up for the day when the florist van cruises up in the nick of time. Red roses aren't my favorite, but they're exactly what I'd expect him to send. Not because he's cliché, but they're the classic choice. And these are primo selection. Upgraded pewter vase, too. Glass would've been fine, prefer-able even, because deep red and pewter is a combination that's hard to look away from—and there's an almost erotic quality to it with the frosty condensation forming. I look again every time I catch a red light. So much for giving me some time.

Nadine calls to check on me. I've held out on her all day, replying to her texts with quick responses because I didn't want to rehash it, but I tell her now about his impromptu coffee delivery, the picture of us online, and the predictable flowers. "He's not going to give up, Oakley."

"He will eventually."

"When's your next therapy appointment?"

"That was subtle."

"Yeah, well, when is it?"

"Tomorrow morning."

"You good tonight?"

"I am. Forget about me and my problems for the rest of the night. Go do filthy things to Jayce that will make him fall madly in love with you."

"He'll be here any minute. But call if you need me."

"I won't." I touch the velvety petals, pluck one to see how it feels, but I regret it immediately, wish I could put it back.

THIRTY

TEAMBUILDING 101

The rest of the week is a blur with two therapy appointments and the usual chaos that is work at this time of year: confirming delivery dates, tracking down deliveries that didn't arrive, booking back-to-back consultations for graduations and engagement parties. June weddings are booked and about to happen, but the wedding consults never cease. We're still a few weeks away from a slowdown and I'll crash when it happens. We all will.

Everything feels status quo until Friday afternoon when Jonna walks into the showroom and says, "I hope you don't have plans tomorrow. We got a last-minute event request and we're all stretched thin so I need you at this one."

"What? We can't pull off something that quickly."

"Oh, yes, we can. This is an important client. And all the wheels are already in motion. All you have to do is be there at eleven-thirty—"

"In the morning?"

"It's pretty damn close to noon. I'm sure you can manage."

"I wasn't objecting to the time itself, just shocked by the timeline. Text me the address."

"You've been there. It's Harold's place."

"Who?"

"The guy with the old dance hall. Rattlesnakes? Pistol in the air? Ringing any bells yet?"

"Who the hell would hold an event there?"

"Client specifically requested some place extremely casual. It's a corporate thing. Wants the employees to be able to blow off some steam and do some team building. All that rah-rah-rah shit."

"Hope these employees are all up-to-date on their tetanus shots."

"We don't question the client's desires."

"We just do whatever it takes to fulfill them. I know." I shake my head in disbelief that someone is actually renting that dump for a corporate event. "Who's the client?"

"Does it matter? Do we treat one client different from the next?"

Damn, somebody's in a mood today. And yes, apparently, we treat this client different because I can't remember ever pulling something together at the last minute for any of our other clients. They book in advance. It's called event planning, not event slap-dash-throw-it-together-ing. "Nope, doesn't matter. I'll be there."

When I pull up to Harold's old barn in the late-morning light, it looks a little better. Not renovated, but refreshed? The siding hasn't been painted but it might have been power washed. And when I walk in, the wood floors have been refinished, there is a new stage at one end, and three ginormous chandeliers hang evenly spaced from heavy beams down the length of the building. It's almost enchanting, the juxtaposition of the elegant lighting with the rest of the rustic interior. The bar is fully functional now and—whoa! *What are the odds he'd be here?*

I approach the bar, and the bartender looks up. "Drink ticket, please."

"I haven't ordered a drink."

"If you plan to, I'm going to need your ticket in advance."

"I wasn't sure you'd remember me."

"Yeah, I remember you." He smiles. "Is that the only sundress you own?"

"Last minute scheduling. The only description I got was casual."

"Well, I don't see how you can play volleyball in it, but I guess it'll work for everything else."

"Volleyball?"

"They've got sand courts in the back. It's pretty nice out there."

Nice? This I need to see with my own eyes. I wander through the back door and my expectations are more than exceeded. There is an expansive wooden deck full of tables and chairs, two sand volleyball courts, a disc golf course at the back, and an open area on the side to pitch washers and play cornhole. This place has sort of an upscale icehouse feel now. Trendy and huge with plenty of parking. I guess Harold knew what he was doing after all.

Speaking of the devil, he walks right up on me. "Well, hello again, Miss Prim."

"Hi, there. You've been busy since I was here last."

"Yeah, but all this was already out here."

"It was?"

"Sure was. But you had your mind made up about this place in less than two shakes. I didn't reckon pestering you to look around a little more was likely to change it."

I glance to the side area where the cornhole boards and washer spikes are set up. "Did you get rid of the rattlesnakes?"

"No more snakes. It's safe."

"Well, I guess I jumped to judgement too quickly. I'm a big enough woman to admit I was wrong."

"Ah, you ain't big enough for shit. Get inside and get a drink, loosen up. You might even have a little fun. The first band's setting up."

"The *first* band?"

"All I can say is this company must really love their employees. It's is all-day and into-the-night affair. Get in there and start enjoying it."

I take Harold's advice and head back inside, back to the bar. "I've decided I'm ready to order. I'm in the mood for a beer. You got a decent amber?"

"You got a drink ticket?"

"I'm event staff. Surely, I don't actually need a ticket."

"You do actually need a ticket."

"Oh, come on. Fine. I'll pay for it."

"Only payment I can take is tickets."

Someone at the end of the bar clears his throat to pull my attention. He holds up a drink ticket when I look his way, uses it to beckon me.

"This is your event? You're the high-maintenance asshole with the last-minute demands?"

He shrugs. I walk down the bar to him. "I guess I should've seen this coming. Yet, here I am, stunned."

"Are you upset because you're not the only one who can surprise someone?"

Why wouldn't Jonna have told me it was him? "I hadn't told them we weren't seeing each other anymore. I guess you took care of that for me."

"If you want something kept a secret, you should clue in everyone affected by it." He sets the drink ticket on the bar, pushes it a few inches toward me, and then looks away as if he doesn't care whether I take it or not.

I snatch it up and wave it at the bartender, make him come to me. When the cold bottle hits the bar top, I thank him. I turn to say thanks to Hollis but I get distracted by a group of guys coming in from the deck, laughing and celebrating a win on the volleyball court. Christian is with them.

"You didn't fire him."

"My HR director sided with you. But he and I had a *clearing the air* session."

"Would not have wanted to be present for that."

"Neither did he. But we got through it. He won't be saying anything offensive to you today. Or ever again."

"Why? Because you told him you'll fire him if he does?"

"I told him I'll break his fucking legs if he does. And I meant it."

"Hollis, you can't threaten your employees like that."

"We met offsite."

"That doesn't make it okay."

"Felt okay to me. In fact, it felt damn good. And my HR director didn't say anything about not doing that."

"You also can't just creatively interpret things to suit your own wants."

"Did you wear that dress for me?"

"I didn't even know you'd be here."

"I prefer to interpret that as a yes."

Dammit. That smile snuck up on me before I could ward it off.

The band starts to play. "Do you want to dance?"

"No." I shake my head, bring my beer to my lips.

He stands and grabs my hand, pulling me forward. "I heard yes."

I barely have time to set my beer back on the bar. "I really don't like this asshole version of you."

"You can make it go away."

"How?"

He pulls me closer until our bodies are pressed together. "Be nice to me and the asshole version will just disappear."

"Or you could be nice on your own so I'll stop seeing you as an asshole."

"Okay, we'll try it your way." He kisses me right here in the middle of an empty dance floor in the middle of a company event where any of his employees could see. And the man just doesn't give a damn. He breaks the kiss to say, "For the record, this dress may be my kryptonite forever. You can probably get me to do anything you want any time you wear it."

"What makes you think we're going to see each other after today?"

"This event doesn't end until ten." He looks at his watch. "It's barely noon. The way I see it, I've got ten hours to win you over. Or wear you down, whatever it takes."

"You're incorrigible."

"I've been told I get like that when I'm in love."

I trip over my feet. Or his feet. Or air—I'm not really sure what just happened. "You don't know me well enough to love me."

"You don't know me well enough to know that I do. But you will." He spins me and all I can see is swirling streaks of light from the chandelier above us. Or maybe it's from the spinning inside my head. Or my chest. Or somewhere lower. I'm not really sure what part of me starting whirling first, but my insides have gone full Rube Goldberg.

We dance. We cash in a few more drink tickets, sit on the deck, sip on beers—alternately smile at something the other has said and stare off at a loss for words. We dance again. Smiles come easier. Ten hours becomes ten minutes.

The event wraps up a little late, but Harold looks like he's on cloud nine, seeing his dancefloor still hopping and people still laughing and talking on the deck. I finally take charge and tell the band to announce that the next song will the their last, and when that song is done, I make sure they don't start another by walking up onto the stage and taking the mic.

"On behalf of Nyx International, I'd like to thank everyone for coming out today, and for allowing J and P Events to put this function together for you. We hope y'all enjoyed yourselves thoroughly but, unfortunately, it's time to call it a night. Please drive safe going home and keep J and P in mind for all your event planning needs."

Hollis helps encourage his employees to head for the parking lot, and then he helps the band load their equipment. "Wow, you're going to great lengths to prove to me you're not really an asshole."

He presses his cheek to mine so no one else can hear. "I'm going to great lengths to get us out of here so I can take you home and fuck you like you've always been mine."

After the band drives away, the only vehicles left in the lot are my car and Harold's truck. "Where's your car?"

"I caught a ride."

"You just assumed I'd drive you home?"

"No, they'd have given me a ride back home if I'd needed it. And you are definitely not driving."

"It's my car."

"But we're going to my house."

"That has no bearing on who drives."

He stops walking, locks his eyes on mine, and threads his fingers into my hair on either side of my face, pulling slightly as he slides them back. "May I drive you home, Oakley Durant?"

"Yes, sir."

Hollis holds his front door open for me, and when I walk through it, the only way I can describe what I feel is to say if a house could hug someone, his just did.

The click of the door shutting behind me seals the welcome with a kiss. He steps behind me and his hands lower the straps of my dress without a word spoken between us. His mouth homes in on my favorite spot at the base of my neck— and this is the kill shot that blows away my hesitation about being with him. The disparities between us will never be bridged; we are not the same, but there is nowhere else I want to be.

He picks me up and carries me to his bedroom, lowers me to his bed, and says, "Take that dress off. And if you're wearing panties, get rid of those, too." While I'm following his orders, he removes his own clothes.

The mattress rearranging under his weight signals a buzz of apprehension, but his body sliding next to mine chases it away. His warm hand caressing between my legs starts to melts my hips in anticipation of his fingers sliding inside me. But he goes off script and slaps all four of his fingers against my pussy, creating a confusing sensation. He watches me to gauge my response. I look up at his searing eyes, seeking access to more of me. "Do that again," I say, my voice faint. When his hand spanks against my vulva again, catching my clit with such a quick, sharp sting, my hips melt entirely, spreading my legs wider. "Don't stop."

His voice is already raw and raspy. "I got you, baby girl. Keep talking to me."

When I tell him to keep going, I assume there will come a point where I'll need what has always worked before—that the slapping will only take me so far. But his repetitive smacks start to leave a vibration of pleasure that's still echoing on my skin when the next strike comes, and before long, I feel a more familiar hum building. *I'm going to come while he's doing this to me. Never in a million years would I have imagined. . .* "Faster."

My one-word direction is all he needs. He intuits how much quicker to strike by watching my body, reading it like only he can. And once again, he makes me feel something no other man ever has. As my orgasm ebbs, he fingers me—not rough but not gentle, somewhere in between that feels just right.

"So tight after just one orgasm," he says, the heady baritone of his voice pinning me to his mattress. "So fucking wet.

I'm going to make you come until I can barely get a finger inside this hungry little snatch, and then I'm going to force-feed it every inch of my hard cock. Watch it stretch around me as I push my way in. Feel these silky walls squeeze me." My glutes and thighs start to quiver, and his devilish smile evokes stronger quakes. "There's my dirty girl. My good girl. Come for me, sweetness." *As if I have a choice.*

He rolls onto his back and he pulls me on top of him. I sit up and squeeze my breasts. "You are exceptionally hot tonight. Such a good little whore—" His face is horror-stricken the moment the word leaves his mouth and his hands grip my hips like he's afraid I'm going to try to flee.

"It's okay," I say. "You can still say it. Only you, but I like it from you."

"I like hearing what you like." His hands relax. His whole body relaxes under me. Well, most of his body. His cock is as hard as I've ever seen it. And we are definitely not waiting until I've had another orgasm for it to be inside me. He doesn't protest when I lift my hips and move into position. "Show me how you like it."

"No," I say. "I'm going to show you how *you* like it." I hold myself open and guide the crown of his erection into place. When I slide down a few inches, I look up to make sure he's watching. "Can you see the way you stretch me from this angle, or do we need to change?"

"Don't change. Just keep going."

THIRTY-ONE

THE FIGHT BEFORE THE FLIGHT

"Pack a toy," he says, watching me from my bedroom doorway.

"What do you mean?"

"You're a grown woman, Oakley. I know you have toys. Pack one."

"Why would you want me to do that?"

"Because I'm secure enough to see those things as team-mates, not opponents. And I want us to have an exceptionally good time on this trip."

"Okay." I reach for my nightstand drawer, and he turns on his heels and tears off toward my kitchen. *I guess he wants it to be a surprise?*

"Shit!" He slams something. A cabinet door? What is he looking for?

I gingerly step out of my room. "Yes, I know I missed the call. I'm sorry but it couldn't be helped. If you can just get him on the line now. Of course, I'll hold." He looks to me and mouths: *I fucked up. I'll make it quick.*

Oh, damn. He missed the call because of me, because I seduced him as soon as his alarm sounded, knowing he had a last-minute contract detail he needed to nail down before we left this morning. I'm the one who fucked up. If he loses a deal over this, I'll never forgive myself. He'll probably never forgive me.

I make myself a cup of tea, sit at the bar, and wait to see how this call turns out. If that deal's blown, there's probably no need to finish packing.

Twenty minutes later, he's laughing and leading me back to my bedroom. "Whew. All's well that ends well."

"Hollis, I'm really sorry."

"For what?"

"I'm the reason you forgot about that call."

"What did I tell you the day we met about apologizing for feeling pleasure?"

"This was hardly the same thing."

"Doesn't matter. It's all fixed. No problem. But if we're going to be ready when the car gets here, I've gotta jump in the shower—" He stops in his tracks and throws his head back. "Well, damn. I forgot to order the car." He unlocks his screen and pulls up a number, hits call, and thrusts the phone at me. "This is the car service I use. When they answer, tell them I need a car to the airport and see if they can make it happen. I may have to drive us." He sprints off to take his shower.

I hold the ringing phone under my chin while I shove another skirt into my bag. "Fuck!" The call disconnects when I drop the phone, and it bounces on the carpet. By the time I retrieve it from under my bed, the screen is locked again. I switch to my phone.

Miracles never cease. I actually score a ride that will get us to the airport on time. This day is looking up, and it can only get better from here.

I'm still finalizing my packing when Hollis appears in the doorway, duffle slung over his shoulder, ready to go. "Are they sending a car?"

"Yeah, but it's not your service. I accidentally disconnected them and your screen locked again, so I just got us an Uber." I grab his phone off the bed and toss it to him.

"Why would you do that?" His breathing sounds labored, as if he's morphing into Darth Vader.

"Because driving to the airport and parking is a hassle."

"You could've come into the bathroom and asked for my PIN to unlock the screen."

"I would've never asked you to tell me your PIN."

"I'd have preferred you do that than pay for the car yourself."

"I have a job. I can pay for a ride to the airport."

"But I didn't intend for you to pay for it. I don't intend for you to pay for anything on this trip."

"Are you being serious right now? Your ego is bruised because I paid for the ride?"

"Don't try to gaslight me into thinking I'm being an asshole."

"Gaslight you? If your first thought is that you're being an asshole, maybe—"

"Stop. I don't want to fight. But from here on out, I pay for this trip. For everything."

My heel is itching to stomp in protest, but I don't want to fight either. The missed phone call and potentially lost deal messed us both up this morning. We're on edge. I take a deep breath. "Okay, agreed." I fan my hand over my open night-stand drawer. "Do you want to pick the toy?"

"If this a peace offering, I'll take it." He steps forward, wearing a Cheshire Cat grin. "Let's go with this."

"Of course, that's the one you'd pick." I laugh, take it from him and nestle it into my clothes.

"Why do you say that?"

"Because of the name."

"What'd you name it?"

"Not me. The company I buy from. All their stuff has ridiculous names. This one is called the *eloquent lover.*"

"Did you just call that thing an elephant plugger?"

"Excuse me!" I know I said the name with my head down but I didn't mumble or slur my words.

"What did you say then?"

"I said el-o-quent love-eerrrr."

"Oh," he nods as if the puzzle pieces have clicked into place, but then he immediately shakes his head. "That doesn't make sense either. What about that thing is eloquent?"

"What about any orifice on my body is like an elephant?"

"Nothing. You're the one who said it."

"No, I said eloquent. You heard elephant. Freudian slip?"

"That applies to things that were actually said, not something being heard incorrectly."

"Oh, my God. Did you eat a big bowl of smug prick flakes while I was in the shower?" My phone dings on the nightstand. He's still standing closest to it. "Will you check that? Shit. I hope our ride's not here already."

He glances at my phone. "I should ignore it. Let them leave, and I'll drive us to the airport." It buzzes again.

I zip my suitcase, tucking in corners of clothing as I go. "Oh, for fuck's sake, will you just check it? I have to pee before we go. My PIN is 8888."

"That's not at all secure."

"Check the damn message!"

I pee quickly and wash my hands like I'm in a race, but he's had plenty of time to read the message by now. He hasn't yelled out to tell me what it was. What the hell is he doing? He still has my phone in his hand when I come back into the room. "Is our ride here?"

"I think I just heard them pull up. But that wasn't the message." He puts my phone in his pocket, picks up my bag, and heads for the front door without another word.

I trail after him. "What was the message?"

He stops at the door with his hand on the knob. "We are going to have such a great time on this trip, Oakley."

"Okay. I hope so. Why are you being weird?"

"I'm not being weird. The message was from Nadine."

"Is she okay?"

"She's fine. Just had a question."

"About what?"

"Someone named . . . Daddy Thick Thighs?" He opens the door and steps outside, leaving me at the threshold, wishing for the ground to swallow me whole. But it won't. And he is never going to let this go. He looks back at me. "Whether you told him you loved him last night . . . or chickened out again."

I wait until he's put our bags in the trunk and gotten into the car before I unglue my feet and force them to move. Buckling myself in, I say, "It's true. I love you."

"Are you sure? Because Nadine seems to think you're in love with some guy named . . . what was it again?"

"Stop."

"Oh, yeah. Daddy Thick Thighs. Is he bigger than me?"

"This is going to be a really long week, isn't it?"

He kisses my forehead. "Oh, yeah. So long. And thick."

My head falls back against the seat. "The thick comment was about your thighs."

"I prefer to interpret that as code for something else."

"Interpret all you want."

He kisses my cheek, and whispers, "Remind me to buy Nadine a present."

"Remind me to break her fingers."

The plane lifts off with his hand on my thigh. And my eyes on his.

EPILOGUE

Six Months Later

"I think this might've been the best party Nyx International has had yet." Hollis twirls me on the dancefloor of the empty hotel ballroom. Everyone else has gone, and we should get out of here. The rental of this space was technically up half an hour ago, not that anyone is waiting to get in here after us.

"Well, we at J and P Events strive to satisfy all our clients' desires." I arch my eyebrow, letting my gaze rake over the perfect fit of his tailored tux.

He drops me into a dip, his eyes mapping the deep V of my vamp-red dress. "I have a few still to be met."

"I'm not on the clock. I'm not contractually obligated to even be nice to you."

His hand is hot on my back as he pulls me up. "I haven't given you your Christmas present yet. You should definitely keep being nice to me."

"Christmas is still two weeks away. I don't know if I can be nice to you for that much longer." I step out of my shoes and carry them as I pull him toward the door.

He's quiet in the elevator up to our room. When he pushes

the door aside and I step past him, the signature scent hits me. The place has grown on me; the free chocolate they regularly send to the showroom has helped. Garth is still trying to figure out what we have to do to get free candles. He's hopeful that my booking the Nyx International holiday party here might've moved the needle. Either way, I'll be his hero because I bought him six of those overpriced candles for Christmas, and I can't wait to give them to him. He's hard to buy for, but I'm confident this year.

Hollis opens his suitcase and pulls out a rumpled gift bag. "Here. This can't wait two more weeks."

"I don't like opening my Christmas presents early."

"Do it for me. Just this once. You'll understand."

I take the bag and remove the tissue to find an ornament. It's an airplane. "Aw. To commemorate our trip to Toronto last summer?"

He smiles and sheds his suit jacket, tossing it at the chair in the corner, not bothering with a hanger or walking it to the closet. "Not quite." He hands me a second bag.

This one holds another ornament: the Eiffel Tower. "Hollis, are you? Are we going to Paris?"

"You told me you could only go if we didn't leave until Christmas Eve and were back in time for New Year's Eve. I hope those dates still work for you because I already booked the trip."

"We're really going to Paris? In less than two weeks?"

"Well, you were looking for a way to get out of spending Christmas with your mom, and you've never been there. We both know how much I love getting to introduce you to new things." He shrugs like it's no big deal. Like booking a trip to Paris is how everyone avoids their family for the holidays.

My mind plays a montage reel of firsts he's introduced me to. Usually at the six-month mark in a relationship, the grand romantic gestures are starting to wane as things become familiar, but Hollis gets more romantic all the time. *Christmas in*

Paris! Sometimes it terrifies me how perfect this feels, but I understand now the difference between being love-bombed and being loved.

"You probably just want to fulfill some fantasy about having your own private, filthy French whore." I start undoing his shirt buttons.

He untucks his shirt while I continue with the buttons. "You're not going to let me down, are you?"

"We'll see." I wink.

"There's an international incident waiting to happen." He removes his cufflinks and slips them into his pocket.

"Stick with me, kid. I'll make you infamous." I slide my hand inside his shirt.

"Can you speak any French?" His skeptical expression makes me wish I could wow him and spew a lengthy answer in the language of love, but my answer is short.

"Oui." I slide both my hands across his chest to open his shirt completely.

"Is that it?"

"Oui."

"Well, if you only know one word, that's a good one." He tosses his shirt to join his jacket on the chair.

My eyes scan for my favorite image in his tattoos, the skull on his forearm, the first one I noticed when he first noticed me and lifted his cup. It always activates that memory, along with my smile. "I bet you say that to all your filthy French whores."

"No. They're all fluent."

"Is that so?" I reach for his belt buckle. "What about you? Are you fluent in filthy French?"

"Oh, yeah. I'm going to say such vile, degrading things to you in Paris, but they'll sound beautiful because they're in French and you won't know the difference." He reaches around for my zipper and pulls it down in one smooth move. My dress pools around my feet. "And all you'll be able to say is 'oui' to my every request."

"Please. You'll be fawning all over me, feeding me butterscotch macarons and buying me silk lingerie and ordering expensive wine."

"And you'll be beautiful." He carries me to the bed. "With croissant crumbs in your hair and cornichons on your breath and pink lipstick prints on your wine glass."

"Yeah, that sounds like me." My back sinks into the plush duvet as he lowers me. "Are you sure you want to take me to Paris?"

"Oui, sweetness." He crawls over me until his forearms frame my face and I'm looking directly up into his smoldering amber eyes. "I want to take you everywhere. Forever."

ABOUT THE AUTHOR

Indie Sparks writes heroines with hutzpah and heroes with dirty mouths and the skills to walk the talk. She gives them all the happy endings they deserve, some for now, some forever. Spicy rom-coms are her favorite flavor in fiction. In real life, she favors the bold, wonderful tastes that some silly urban legend calls bitter and insists makes her more prone to becoming a serial unaliver. She wouldn't hurt anyone, but she would gladly take everyone's black coffee, red wine, and extra-dark chocolate. Her purse holds more lipsticks than money, and the only thing bulging more than her bookshelves is the men in her books.

MORE TITLES BY INDIE SPARKS

Peri

She was the wildest girl in town. He was the boy with the strongest
arm and the truest aim. The rebel child and the golden
boy. Together, they were hell-bent for chaos. Who was the match and
who was the gasoline? Depended on the day. But that was a long
time ago.

On My Merry Way

She may not have put "sexy stranger" on her Christmas list, but
Santa knows what a good girl needs to make her holiday complete.
Who knew one wrong-number text could turn out so right? Light the
fireworks and pour the champagne! The naughty list is ready to make
merry.

Modern Life of a Vintage Brat

She's an independent brat, who owns a vintage boutique. He's the
smoking hot owner of the cigar bar next door, who is accustomed to
being in control. She's not looking to be tamed, but she has no
objection to him trying.

Steamy Rom-Com Duologies from INDIE SPARKS

VENGEFUL VIXENS:

Your Boss Says Hi!

(the book you just read)

Your Trainer Says Hi!

She only wants to see her ex's beloved personal trainer in the gym—until he convinces her his hot tub could do wonders for her aching muscles. He isn't wrong, but between the heat, the bubbles, and his off-the-clock skills, she might be in too deep before she knows it. He's definitely not her type. So, why can't she stop seeing him?

NAUGHTY AT THE NOUVEAU:

Maintenance & Management

She's the new property manager. He's the new maintenance supervisor. They rub each other the wrong way . . . until they start to rub each other the right way. There's a non-fraternization policy, so they really shouldn't. But there's only one bed!

Landscaping & Leasing

He ghosted her after an unfortunate incident that she had absolutely no control over—and now, she's accidentally hired his landscaping company. She may not be completely immune to his charms (that voice!), but she's not weak enough to fall for him twice. But what if she doesn't know the whole story about why he disappeared from her life?